"I think it's time you come clean."

Her hands continued to shake.

Wilder's eyes softened as he led her to the table and into a chair. She didn't want this—this feeling of needing him. But part of her relished that he was here. Protecting her. It wrapped around her heart and caressed it until it was warm and pliable. No. She closed her eyes. She would not let herself react this way to him.

"Cosette?" Wilder sat across from her, leaned forward on the table. "Did he hurt you?"

"No. I think I scared him. Interrupted him."

"Interrupted him doing what?" His voice was low and icy.

"Drawing that heart. Sifting through my things." She couldn't stop shaking.

Wilder got up from the table and pulled her into his powerful arms. "How long has this been going on?"

Cosette couldn't keep this a secret any longer. Wilder would lose all faith in her when he discovered the truth that she wasn't the put-together professional he thought her to be. "The first time or this time?"

Wilder stiffened.

Jessica R. Patch lives in the mid-South, where she pens inspirational contemporary romance and romantic suspense novels. When she's not hunched over her laptop or going on adventurous trips with willing friends in the name of research, you can find her watching way too much Netflix with her family and collecting recipes for amazing dishes she'll probably never cook. To learn more about Jessica, please visit her at jessicarpatch.com.

DANGEROUS OBSESSION

JESSICA R. PATCH

HARLEQUIN® LOVE INSPIRED® SUSPENSE

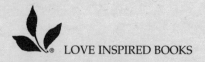

PLEASE RECYCLE
THIS PRODUCT IS RECYCLABLE

Recycling programs
for this product may
not exist in your area.

LOVE INSPIRED BOOKS

ISBN-13: 978-1-335-49044-5

Dangerous Obsession

Copyright © 2018 by Jessica R. Patch

www.Harlequin.com

Printed in U.S.A.

Fear not: for I have redeemed thee,
I have called thee by thy name; thou art mine.
–Isaiah 43:1

To my sister, Celeste. The love you have for people
who are hurting and your gift to help them always
amazes me. I admire and respect you and your calling.
Also, thank you for the invaluable information in helping
me plot this story—I'm not sure which one of us
is creepier. Let's blame Mom either way!

Special thanks to:
My agent, Rachel Kent. My editor, Shana Asaro.
And my brainstorming partner, Susan Tuttle.

ONE

*I've missed you. When you visit the one you love,
you'll see how much I love you, too.*

Cosette LaCroix's hands trembled and she dropped the
card with the typed note inside on the café table. It had
been three years and she'd finally stopped looking over
her shoulder, waiting for Jeffrey Levitts—her former
boyfriend and boss in Washington, DC—to appear. But
he'd found her. And she knew exactly what this note
meant. She darted a glance out the large café windows
and searched the sidewalks. Was he out there lurking?
She shivered, suddenly feeling watched.

"Hey!" Wilder Flynn's husky, deep voice boomed.

Cosette startled and fumbled to shove the card inside
the envelope and appear calm. Collected. Her present
boss couldn't know about Jeffrey—that she'd been in a
relationship with a narcissistic monster. Her job was to
spot these people. To help other women escape them.
Not fall into the same trap. Not to mention Wilder didn't
know she'd taken the job at Covenant Crisis Management three years ago to escape Jeffrey. Who better to
find safety with than a security specialist? She was supposed to be one herself!

Clearing her throat, she masked the sheer terror sending her heart into arrhythmia. "What?" she barked and
balled her fist in her lap to conceal the tremors.

He cocked his head, studied her and frowned. "Amy

said you took the last of the cascara syrup. I was set on a cascara latte. It's been a rough morning."

"Couldn't find any matching socks?" Cosette smirked, but inside she was drowning. She peeked out the window again, watching downtown Atlanta in action and hoping Jeffrey wasn't out there. "Tell Aurora to order more syrup." Aurora Marsh had opened Sufficient Grounds 2.0 a year ago, after her first coffee café had burned down, when she'd lived in Hope, Tennessee. Cosette loved the atmosphere here. Wilder loved the free coffee and free use of the conference center to meet with clients and colleagues on occasion, which must be why he was here.

"Matching socks have nothing to do with it. I'm trying to figure out what to do with the apartment upstairs now that you've moved out—which I still think is ridiculous." He pouted like a child, not a six-foot-three former Navy SEAL who ran a world renowned private security company. Wilder collapsed in the chair across from her, his ebony hair falling over his eyebrows. He didn't keep a military cut like most soldiers. Probably because one of his best features was his thick, luxurious locks. It was shaggy, but not like a kid who needed a haircut. More like a hair model. She'd love to run her hands—

"Stop staring at my hair and focus." Teasing played in his voice.

"I'm not staring." But taking her mind off what was lying on the table helped bring calm to her jittery insides. Nothing helped the feeling that malicious eyes might right now be spying on her, though.

He gave her a pointed look. Okay, she was staring. Wilder was a sight to behold, but she'd given up on men for good after Jeffrey. Men in her life abused and manipulated, all the way back to her father, who was rotting in a New Orleans prison this very moment. Right where he belonged. The thought brought her back to the card, and her stomach knotted.

"What's going on with you?" Wilder asked, his usual charm replaced with concern. Great. She thought she'd done a better job hiding it.

"Nothing," she managed.

"Look at me." Wilder waited and she inhaled, then slowly shifted her gaze to his emerald greens canopied by dark lashes. He peered into her eyes until she squirmed in her seat. It felt like a year passed with him just staring at her, searching for truth, assessing. "You're lying to me," he murmured.

She didn't want to. "I'm not." He was going to push until she squealed. That was his way, which wasn't fair. Wilder was sealed tighter than his weapons' cage at CCM. He would never take the hourly couch sessions she required from all team members. Never talked about his sister Meghan's murder—and it had been several years since she'd been killed by a stalker. Cosette felt the blood drain from her face in a whoosh.

"Yes, you are, Cosette. You're looking me right in the eye and lying your face off." His inhalation was sharp and he pushed back in his chair. "But I guess we're all entitled to secrets. I just don't like ones that bleach your face and make you fidgety and paranoid."

She didn't like keeping secrets from Wilder, but she would have to admit she'd originally accepted the job to hide. From a stalker! Admit she'd failed professionally… and personally. "I, um…I got an invitation to my fifteenth high school reunion." One truth she could reveal.

How did Jeffrey know her PO box number? She never used her physical address.

"Really? That's what's got your pants in a wrinkle?" The black-as-night scruff that covered Wilder's chin, cheeks and neck hid a face that was too boyish to be thirty-three, but it didn't hide the fact he wasn't buying her weak excuse.

No, that wasn't what had her in a mood; she wasn't going. While Jeffrey had been the most humiliating "relationship" of her life, since she ought to have seen the signs—she was a behavioral expert!—it wasn't her only disastrous or toxic romance. With an abusive father came all the baggage. And as a teenage girl, she'd wanted approval, acceptance and love. She'd been like a starving dog, happy to eat scraps. It had led to many rotten boys. She would no more step foot at that reunion, where people knew her indiscretions, her poor family history, than—

"Are you going?" Wilder was holding her postcard-style invitation in his hand, pointing to the Plus-One. "It's this weekend."

She always visited Mama's grave on Mother's Day. That was next Sunday. But Jeffrey had left something there for her and he'd be expecting her to come retrieve it—or he might be baiting her. If she used the reunion as a cover, she could go early and still pay Mama her respects, as well as change the flowers on her grave.

"If I can have the weekend, including Friday, off." Working in the security industry meant her weekends were often tied up on the job.

"You want both weekends off?" He raised an eyebrow.

"No, I'll just visit my mama's grave this Sunday."

Wilder's lips corkscrewed and his eyes narrowed. "What's the real deal with you, Cosette?" He folded his arms and pinned her with a glare. *This man!*

"Nothing. I just… I need this weekend."

"And a Plus-One." He held up the invitation again and pointed to it.

She groaned. "I don't need a man."

Men were nothing but trouble. Possessive. Demanding.

A lopsided grin spread. "Well, what about a chicory coffee? Because I need that cascara latte."

She wasn't immune to Wilder's ways. His charm was like a weapon he wielded with ease and perfection, always hitting his intended target. But she *was* wise to it and right now, he wanted her to relax so she'd spill the truth. Also, he did want her latte. That much she would give in to.

She slid him the coffee. "I have lipstick marks on it."

"Red." He didn't bother to wipe the stains away before he sipped the drink. "My favorite." The way he said it—the action itself—did strange things to her belly. No. Way. Wilder was a gorgeous man, honest and caring, but there were too many reasons she refused to entertain romantic ideas about him. He had a few traits that kept her at bay, like his obsessive tendencies and his need to control, plus he was her boss, and if that wasn't enough, he was emotionally unavailable. Besides, she wasn't going to be another man's possession ever again. "When do we leave Friday?" he asked.

"There is no 'we'—only me." The last thing she needed was Wilder forcing her to attend the reunion and discovering what a needy, clingy and starved-for-love girl Cosette had been—might still be. "And if you're going to drink my latte, the least you can do is go order my chicory coffee." She shooed him away with her hand. She needed air. A minute to think without him hovering.

His massive frame lifted from the chair and he swaggered to the counter, his trendy jeans fitting snugly and his white dress shirt stretching across his back.

Should she even go to New Orleans at all? She didn't care that Jeffrey had left her something at the grave— no, she did. It angered her that he would infringe on her private place where she honored her mother. He'd desecrated it. And he wasn't going to keep her from going to Mama like she did every year.

"Here's your coffee with chicory, Miss LaCroix." Amy grinned and set it on the table. "Mr. Flynn had a phone call. Said to deliver it to you in person because…" her cheeks turned pink "…you were too lazy to walk to the counter and get it yourself. I think he was teasing, though."

Cosette rolled her eyes and darted one last peek out the window, trying not to shiver again. "Thanks, Amy. And how many times do I have to tell you to call me Cosette?" Amy had been dating their computer analyst for almost five months. By now, they should be on a first name basis. She motioned to Wilder's empty chair. "Have a seat if you have a sec." She could use a distraction from the card, from the feeling of eyes on her, from Wilder.

Amy sat across from her, a dreamy grin on her face.

"Thinking of Wheezer?" Cosette asked. She knew that lovesick look.

"We're going ice-skating tonight at the indoor rink."

Wheezer didn't seem like the skating type. It was nice to see Amy bringing him out of his shell and the control room at CCM. He lived on computers and was a cyber genius. The things he could do with a computer were scary.

"That sounds fun. You ready to be done with school for the summer? Any big plans?"

Amy shook her head. "I'm spending it with my mom."

"That's great." Cosette's heart pinched. She'd give anything to go on a summer trip with her mom. To hug her or even hold her hand just one more time. "Enjoy the time you have. It's precious." And fleeting. If Mama had listened to Cosette and left Dad, she'd still be alive. But she was the textbook case of an abused wife. Cosette's training and begging hadn't been enough to save her—to convince her she could walk away.

Her phone rang. Her dad's lawyer calling again. She ignored every single one. She didn't care what he had to say. The phone beeped notifying her that she had a voice mail. She promptly deleted it without listening, as she had all of them in the past few months. She'd never forgive her father for what he'd done. Never betray her mother in that way.

The scripture that encouraged loving and forgiving your enemies needled her, but she ignored it.

Sorry, Lord, this one is too hard.

Wilder returned and Amy stood. "Back to work."

He reclaimed his uninvited spot. "Okay, what time are we leaving Friday?"

Cosette snorted and sifted through a few ads, folding the ones she wanted and tucking them into her purse. "Don't you have something better to do?"

"Other than the crew coming out to go Karate Kid on the house, I'm dead-free."

"Painters or they're kicking it down?"

Wilder didn't bother to answer. He checked his phone. Sent a text. "Time?"

He wasn't going to let it go. Why wasn't he going to let it go?

Because she was a terrible liar. She knew all the tricks and she still stank at it. She was a fraud through and through, and Wilder was onto her. His intuition was practically perfect. Like some kind of otherworldly power. Probably what kept him alive on so many tours and SEAL missions. Too bad her intuition wasn't that spot-on. She might never have been involved with Jeffrey—or numerous others before him.

The more she protested, the worse it would become.

Wilder's obsessive tendencies wouldn't allow him to let up. But he wasn't a sociopath or a narcissist. Actually, he was the only man she felt truly, completely safe with—physically. She didn't trust her heart to anyone but herself these days. No getting out of this. Looked like she was stuck attending the reunion.

"Do we fly or drive?" she asked.

"Do we want to get there in less than two hours or less than seven?"

She didn't want to get there at all. But if she was going to visit Mama's grave, this was her sliver of opportunity. "Less than two. I'll book a flight. Festivities start at seven."

Wilder stood and lightly brushed her shoulder as he leaned down. "Wear your dancin' shoes, darlin'," he murmured, drawing out the endearment like he always did in a soft, Southern purr, then he left the café. She rubbed the gooseflesh on her arms.

This was a stupid and dangerous idea on so many levels.

Wilder didn't believe a word that came out of the French Cajun's mouth. A very kissable mouth coated in cherry red. Something in that stack of mail the other day had wigged her out and in the three years Wilder had known Cosette, very little scared her. He admired that—her strength and bravery. Her cool head and soothing voice, unless she had her dander up and then she'd go to town jabbering in French Cajun—not one word understandable, but he sure enjoyed watching it. Enjoyed watching her in general. Graceful. Poised. That long, brunette hair wavy and wild down her back. But that's all he could do—admire and appreciate.

He didn't date team members. But that wasn't the main

reason he couldn't pursue his attraction to her. An attraction that had almost kept him from hiring her altogether. In that initial interview, there had been desperation in her eyes—like that of a wounded animal, horror-struck and terrified. Like she needed to come under his sheltering wings. So he'd said yes. Her credentials were top-shelf, but the pull toward her...that was visceral and scary. Wilder didn't have the luxury of falling in love.

He had his people to protect and lead.

Clients who needed his attention.

And mostly, if he gave his heart away, he'd have to give it all, which meant transparency and honesty about his past. That was something he wasn't willing to give. If Cosette knew the deep secrets he harbored, she'd lose all respect for him. All trust. That terrified him more than his attraction to her. So he kept her at arm's length. But it wasn't easy. And this weekend was a dumb idea, but something had her rattled and she'd barely spoken on the flight to New Orleans. Not taking two weekends off sent a red flag flying; she'd made sure she was at her mother's grave every Mother's Day since she'd taken the job. Had noted in her interview that it was important to her. She'd rather go to her reunion and swing by the gravesite a week early? Nope. He hadn't bought it. Too bad he hadn't gotten his hands on her mail. Federal offense, but Wilder wasn't above crossing lines if it meant protecting the people he cared about.

She'd said to meet him in the hotel lobby at six. He grabbed his keys, wallet and phone and headed that way. She sat on a bar stool drinking a soda and looking absolutely stunning. Glad not to be wearing a tie, he felt choked already. He leaned against the bar and tapped her shoulder, startling her. Her head was somewhere else.

Fear coursed through those coffee-bean-colored eyes. Her smile didn't reach them.

But he'd let it go. For now.

"You ready, Miss LaCroix?" He extended his elbow and she accepted and slid off the stool, reaching him at chin-level in her sleek red heels. "You look incredible."

She snorted and adjusted her snug but not too revealing dress. "Puh-leeze."

Cosette wasn't what he'd call model thin, but then he thought those women needed a roast beef sandwich. He liked her curves.

They drove to a nearby park. The pavilion had been decorated in strands of twinkling white lights and a live band played. Cosette opted out of name tags. Newspaper stretched across a long table and mounds of crawfish, corn on the cob, shrimp and baby potatoes spilled from one end to the other. Wilder's mouth watered.

Cosette filled her plate, but she wasn't herself. Nervous. Fidgety. Distracted. Head down, making zero eye contact with people.

Wilder didn't like it. Didn't like that worry and fear in her eyes. He scanned the scene. Booze flowed and smoke drifted on the warm Southern air. His instincts went on high alert. Something eerie wafted with the laughter and Cajun spices.

"You want to sit over at that picnic table?" he asked.

"Sure."

A few women stopped her and chatted. Typical female jest. They grinned, but sized one another up. Who'd gained more weight? Who had the better job? The better man? As if it wasn't obvious. He was a man and could see it. *Women.* Wilder shook his head, but smiled as Cosette introduced him.

They gawked at his hair.

He ought to cut it. But he had to admit—to himself and no one else alive—he loved his hair. No reason. Just did.

They moseyed to the table as the New Orleans jazz band played. People whirled on the gazebo dance floor. But Cosette was not into this night. "So how bad did you hate high school?" he asked.

She pinched the mudbug and sucked the juice out, then went to work on the tail like a pro. That was one thing Wilder could not do. "Bad," she said and dived into another one. "But I worked my behind off so I could get scholarships for college. Get educated…get out."

"Why are you here then?" Maybe he'd get to the truth. Probably not. Cosette was working pitifully hard to conceal something. She wasn't bound to crack anytime soon, and ribbing her would only prolong it. And yet he couldn't help himself. The deep desire to know, to protect, to fix whatever ailed her nagged him half to death.

"I miss the music."

"Pandora station right there on your phone."

"I like my music live."

"Buy a live album."

She scowled and ignored his remark. He peeled his shrimp and ate. Spicy enough to open his sinuses.

Several more former students made their way to the table and chatted with Cosette. Every time, she seemed afraid, and she never stopped scanning the woods, the crowds. Finally, after eating a piece of key lime pie, she excused herself to the restroom, and Wilder went straight for the cherry crisp. She hadn't returned by the time he'd eaten that and drunk a cup of punch, so he strode toward the restrooms and caught a blonde coming out.

"Have you seen Cosette? Cosette LaCroix?" Something was wrong, burning his gut like acid, and it wasn't the Cajun food.

"She's not in there." A sly grin slid across the woman's face. "I think I saw her talking to Beau Chauvert earlier. She may have slipped off with him. Old Beau—in many ways. But she'd be crazy to go with him. Not with a man like you at her side."

Wilder wanted to say "Go home, lady, you're drunk." But she'd probably think it was full of innuendo. "Thanks," he said instead and darted behind the restrooms. Where could she be? He knew Cosette well enough to know she wouldn't slip into the dark with any man willingly.

"Beau! Let go of me!" Cosette hollered as her high school boyfriend hauled her farther into the woods. She clawed at his beefy arms, sickened at his booze-laced breath.

"I just wanted to talk to you. To dance. I've missed you."

Her blood froze. The first line in the note she'd received... Did she have it all wrong? Had Beau sent the card?

"But you don't want to talk. Or dance with the likes of me. I'm not good enough for you now." He shoved her against a tree. "I used to be very good for you."

Cosette's stomach roiled and the bark dug into the thin fabric of her dress.

"You are lookin' so fine. Little thicker than I remember, but I'm not complaining."

"Beau," she said, trying to remain calm. To see him as a hostile patient. "You're drunk. Why don't you sleep it off, and we can talk tomorrow when you're sober. I'm in town a couple more days." But she wouldn't be seeing him, that was for sure.

He released his grip and she stepped away from the tree, her heart racing. She slowly backed out of the woods.

Beau stepped forward and grabbed her forearm. She'd

have bruising tomorrow. "You think you're all uppity now? I know what you really are."

Brush and twigs snapped.

Cosette would recognize the imposing figure a mile away.

"You have less than a second to take your hands off her," Wilder said, his voice low and menacing. The man could be boyish and charming, and in an instant, menacing and terrifying. It sent a zing into her middle.

Beau was a bully. This wouldn't end well—for Beau.

"And just what are you gonna do about it?" he spat, spittle landing in dots on Cosette's neck.

In a blink, Wilder had inserted himself between the two of them. He faced Beau, put his palm flush against Cosette's belly and guided her behind him, leaving his hand resting against her. The feel of his warmth seeping through the fabric of her dress brought her comfort as well as butterflies.

"When I was in fourth grade, two sixth grade bullies would take my milk money. Every. Single. Day."

Where in the world was this going?

"You know what I did about it?"

Uh-oh.

"Nothing."

Beau chuckled. "And you're gonna do nothin' about this, either. This is between me and my old lady."

Wilder's face appeared relaxed, except for that one little tick in his jaw when Beau called her his. She wasn't his. She belonged to nobody but herself.

Wilder cocked his head, pressed his hand more firmly into her belly as he guided her another step back. "The reason I did nothing wasn't out of fear. I didn't care because...I just don't like milk."

"Wilder," Cosette whispered. Now was not the time for one of his many anecdotes.

"But then they started bullying the milk money from my sister Meghan, and Meghan loved her chocolate milk. Every day at one fifteen. So I had to get involved. Because she was my baby sister and I cared about her."

Uh-oh. His voice had changed. Become deeper. Sinister. He was going to—

He wrenched Beau's arm behind his back and slammed him face-first into a tree. Beau cried out. "Now, if I apply just a bit more pressure—" Wilder said.

Beau cried out again.

"—your elbow's gonna break. It's excruciating. Or you can apologize to the lady—who doesn't belong to you and is far from old—and not only leave the area but the event. Do you understand?"

"Yeah. Yeah." Beau nodded profusely.

By now, a small crowd had gathered. Cosette's cheeks heated.

"And don't drive drunk." He let up on Beau. Beau turned and swung.

Wilder grabbed his fist and put him on the ground, then planted his foot on Beau's back like a weight. "Can one of you spectators come take this jerk home before he gets himself killed?"

Not that Wilder would kill him. But he was furious. A cold and quiet kind of fury. She'd seen it before. Much more frightening than someone blowing a gasket.

One of Beau's old buddies stepped up. "I—I can."

Wilder raked his hand through his hair and put his arm around Cosette. "Let's go buy a red velvet cake and two forks." He said it as if he hadn't just been involved in an altercation.

"That's my favorite cake," she said and leaned into

him as they blew past her gaping classmates, loathing herself for resting in his strength and comfort. She didn't want to need him or have these feelings stirring inside her. Wilder gave her security, and if she lapped it up, she'd be a lost puppy. Nope. Not happening. Time to get a handle on her feelings ASAP.

"I know." He led her to the parking lot as crickets chirped. Music continued to play in the distance, and her heart thumped to a beat she refused to register.

Wilder opened the car door for her, but blocked her from getting inside. "I don't understand. If this guy scares you so bad, why did you bother to come? You've barely spoken to anyone. And did you really date that mule?"

Cosette hung her head, humiliation and shame flushing her face. If he thought Beau was bad, he'd really look down on her for Jeffrey.

Wilder tipped up her chin. "Hey, look at me… We all have exes from our teenage years we wish we didn't. But you could have done so much better."

Back then, she didn't believe that. And now? Now she just wanted to be alone even if it was lonely.

He brushed his thumb across her jawline. "Are you hurt?"

"No," she whispered. "I'm fine." Now. Thanks to Wilder.

"He won't bother you again. I'll make sure of that."

Cosette believed him. But what about the real threat out there? The cunning and manipulative man who lurked in the shadows and hid behind his PhD? Or was Beau the real threat? If he wasn't the original danger, after the humiliation, he would be one now. The thought hung over her like a thick blanket of cold darkness and she shivered.

"Is there anything else I need to know, Cosette?"

He must be getting that superhero hunch. She swallowed the truth, choking on it. "No. No, I'm fine."

For now.

* * *

"Do you want me to come with you?" Wilder asked.

Cosette gripped the door handle of the rental car and stared out at the sea of tombstones marking the lives of loved ones. "No." She did this alone every year. She'd never feared coming, though. Until now. "I know some people would say that she's not there—not really. And I know that. She's in heaven with Jesus. But it comforts me to come. To talk to her as if she's alive. To clean up the weeds and replace the flowers. I've—I've even brought a blanket before and spent a whole afternoon."

"Would you like to do that now? I can come back for—"

"No!" She choked down the fear. Jeffrey might be out here, hidden in the woods, watching and waiting. Or Beau. With no car, no Wilder… She couldn't risk being stranded. And that's how she felt. Stranded. Alone. Hedged in. She forced a pleasant expression. "I mean… no, thanks."

The lines in Wilder's brow deepened and he searched the cemetery as if scanning for threats. "I'll be here. Stay as long as you like. I have a book."

"You're reading a book?" She bit down on her lip and smirked. "I mean, I'm not implying…" She sighed. Wilder was well-educated, he just didn't like much fiction. Most military suspense wasn't believable, according to him. "I—"

"How about I pull you up out of that gigantic hole you just dug?" His grin lit up and warmed a few dark and empty places within her. "It's by a former SEAL. Not rocket science." He tugged a strand of her hair. "Go on. Go talk to your mama."

"Thank you, Wilder. For everything. Even the cake, though I certainly don't need it." She was five-eight and wore size twelve. "Hippie chick" brought a whole new meaning when coupled with her. In today's society, she'd be a plus-size model! Okay, enough self-hatred over weight. She had other things to hate herself for that were far worse.

"Cake looks good on you." He held up his book and motioned with his chin for her to get going.

She exited the vehicle and weaved slowly through the cemetery. Memories of her and Mama cooking, baking, shopping, sunbathing, filled her mind. Cosette missed her so. If only she would have left for safety's sake.

He loves me, Cosie.

You don't know him. He doesn't mean to do it.

He's sorry. Really. Deep down he's a good man.

He's had a terrible life. If you only knew...

One excuse after another to defend Dad. Cosette wiped a tear and stood before Mama's grave. She clasped her throat. Someone had already replaced the old flowers with a bouquet of white tulips. Cosette dropped to her knees and yanked them out of the vase. Jeffrey would not get this pleasure.

Then she saw a small black velvet box buried in the weeds. Her lungs turned to brick.

Hands trembling, she picked up the box and opened it. Inside were a pair of pink tourmaline earrings. Round. Simple. Cosette scanned the secluded cemetery, finding its hallowedness and peacefulness gone. Jeffrey had ruined this. She hung her head and sobbed, fear rising in her throat and leaving her dizzy and angry...so angry that he would do this. Wreck this one place she held dear. That's when she saw the slip of paper.

She wiped her eyes and removed it from the box.

I'll always love you.

Would she ever be rid of this man? Why would he

come back after two years of being quiet? It wasn't like she'd used cash or changed her name. She'd blocked him from her cell phone, but she hadn't changed the number; her patients might need her, and she wanted to be available to each one of them.

If he'd hired a PI, it wouldn't have taken this long to track her to Atlanta. Something must have triggered him. She wadded up the note and dropped the earrings in her purse.

Lord, I know You're probably not listening much to me, since I'm unwilling to forgive my dad—You know where I stand on that. But please, please don't let this turn into what it was in Washington. Please!

She searched the tree line. Had she evaded his trap by coming early? If he was in Atlanta, following her, wouldn't he know she'd left for the airport two days ago?

"Sorry to cut things short, Mama, but I'm in real trouble here and I'm scared." Scared she'd end up lying right next to her. Because Cosette would never surrender to Jeffrey and it would eventually bring him to a vengeful state. He'd try to kill her before it was over. And if Beau had decided to come after her...she was in a heap of trouble.

"I love you, Mama, but I gotta go." She kissed her fingertips and placed them on Mama's headstone, then scurried back to the car.

Wilder scowled. "I've read maybe ten pages and I'm not a slow reader. What's up?"

"Nothing. I'm ready to go."

A dark eyebrow arched and he held her gaze a beat longer than she liked, but then he motioned to the passenger seat. "We have time to kill before we have to be at the airport. You hungry?" he asked.

Not even a little bit. "Sure."

They chose a restaurant near the airport.

Inside, at their table, he said, "When Caley was about six, she climbed a tree. She'd watched me and Meghan do it earlier. Mama told her not to. But hey, she was six and had something to prove."

Good grief. Another anecdote.

"But she fell and skinned her knee and bloodied her nose. You picking up what I'm putting down?"

"Stay out of trees?"

He huffed. "If you keep trying to hide whatever's got you scared…you'll end up bloodied. Don't wreck that pretty face by falling on it."

He wasn't far from the truth. She might very well end up exactly as he said. She didn't want to run again, and anyway, where would she go? She was safest with Wilder. Not telling him might get him hurt. But she wasn't sure what scared her most: admitting the truth, Beau Chauvert or Jeffrey Levitts.

"If you don't want to talk about it, fine. I don't like it. I probably won't keep quiet for long. But right now, you can eat in peace. Talk about something else."

"Are you letting it slide because you know I'll expect you to reciprocate and give me therapy time? Fair is fair, after all."

"Nothing about life is fair, Cosette." Wilder ran his finger down the menu, browsing. "And the difference is I don't need to talk. I'm not scared. You most definitely are, which means there's a threat out there. I can make that go away for you."

"What happened to eating in peace?" She couldn't even concentrate on the menu. Nothing appealed to her stomach, but when the server returned she ordered the salmon and jasmine rice.

"I also said I probably wouldn't keep quiet for long."

His playful smirk loosened some of the nerves bundled in her chest and she breathed deep. Decided to switch subjects.

"I do want to talk to you about one thing." It had been on her mind for the past few months. "Equine therapy."

"I don't want to lay on your couch and blabber, and I don't want to ride horses to soothe my soul. I'm solid."

Cosette unrolled her silverware and placed the linen napkin in her lap. "I'm talking about reconstructing and expanding that stable on the plantation, putting up fencing and opening an equine therapy practice. I'd get a loan and take care of the costs, and pay you rent, of course."

"I don't know, Cosette. People trying to heal on the same property as people who are in serious trouble sometimes... That might put them at risk."

"I've thought of that, but we rarely have serious risks, and it's far enough from the main house. I could even add an office area off the stables for more privacy, and have a road paved so clients could bypass the main house altogether... And if something dangerous is happening then I can cancel."

"Five months ago, a sniper tried to take out Evan. He shot through the guest bedroom window. We didn't know it was dangerous until it was. Remember that?"

Yes, she'd been at the clinic where she worked part-time when that happened. "Wilder, please consider it. I've written up a proposal and I'll give you some information to help you understand how important this is. Patients are making great strides with this kind of therapy and the plantation is such a peaceful and lovely place."

"Yet you moved out."

Cosette finally felt like Jeffrey's reign of terror had ended and she was safe. Now with Jody moved out, since she and Evan were married, it was odd living upstairs while Wilder lived downstairs. "Just think about it. I'll give you the information when we get back into town."

"Fine."

The drive and boarding the plane were relatively quiet between them. Cosette pretended to read on the flight, but her mind was a muddied mess. What would come next? By the time they landed and retrieved their baggage, it was late. Wilder drove to her apartment, brooding. He pulled up in a visitor parking space. "You want me to come in?"

"Why would I want that?" *Yes!*

He gripped the steering wheel and sighed. "I guess I don't know." He hauled her bags to her door. "I'll see you in the morning."

"Yes. Good. Okay." She unlocked her door and Wilder gently grasped her arm.

"Cosette, you can tell me anything. You know that, right?"

"And you can tell me anything but you never do." This man needed to open up. To talk out his feelings. Bottled up emotions eventually blew. With everything he'd seen being a SEAL, and his job, and the death of his sister, there was plenty for Wilder to discuss, to air out. Why wouldn't he trust her?

"*Anything*... Okay, I'll tell you something I've never shared with anyone."

Finally.

"I'm vain about my hair. I know I'm a soldier and, you know, a legit tough guy...but I just like my hair." He grinned, all charming like. It almost worked. She felt the smile forming deep in her heart, but caught it before it reached her lips.

"Well, yippee skippy, you're vain. You've failed miserably at keeping *that* a secret. Everybody already knows it." She rolled her eyes and pushed open the door. Wilder was far from vain, but it was obvious he cared about his hair. Though he didn't flip it around or mess with it much... Well, he did comb his hands through it often. She assumed that was an anxious habit, or frustration. Maybe he just liked the feel.

"I'll come up with something better tomorrow," he deadpanned and flashed a commercial-worthy grin. But she was going into a dark and empty home—one she hoped was empty—so the grin fell flat.

"You do that." Before he could respond, she hurried inside. Not that she wanted to be there, but she didn't want to spar with Wilder—not when he was all flirty and enamoring. She was at war for her life with a stalker. She didn't need to be at war for her heart with her boss. A cold chill swept up her spine. *It's fine.* She was fine. Cosette flipped on a light. Nothing out of place. She rolled her bag into her bedroom.

She needed a long hot bath and a good night's sleep.

Creak!

Cosette's muscles locked up and her heart skittered into her throat.

She was hearing things. No one was in her house.

Blood pulsed in her ears, making a whooshing noise like a ceiling fan. It hurt to breathe. She listened. Nothing.

Letting out a relieved breath, she reached for the light switch.

Something rustled in her closet.

Her hand froze on the switch. She couldn't move. Couldn't flip on the light. Couldn't breathe.

Suddenly, the closet door burst open and a figure charged through the darkness, knocking her into the chest of drawers and sending her crashing to the floor as he exited her bedroom. She lay there in terror, unable to form a coherent thought. But she couldn't lie here all night. Where did he go? Would he be back? She forced clarity to come, and after a moment, gasped and flipped on the light, while pain throbbed in her shoulder.

Her vanity stool had been knocked over, as if the dark-clad figure had tripped, hurrying to the closet to conceal himself before being caught red-handed. But doing what? She slowly searched her bedroom, her heart racing like a meteor. Her makeup was out of place. Something drew her attention to the mirror, and she clasped her burning throat. Drawn in lipstick on her vanity mirror was a huge heart.

Invisible creepy-crawlers skittered across her skin.

"Hey."

Cosette screamed and grabbed the vase on her dresser, spinning to face her attacker.

Wilder held his palms up, gun in one hand. "Hey," he repeated softly, soothingly. "It's just me." He inched toward her and slowly removed the vase from her grasp. "I had a feeling I needed to come back. Your front door was unlocked. Why didn't you…" His glance took in the vanity mirror. "Is he still here?" He'd connected the dots.

She shook her head.

"Lock this behind me." Like a bullet from a gun, he was out the front door.

Cosette did as he commanded, concentrating on breathing, but the lipstick heart was a huge menacing sign that Jeffrey had returned. In her home! She went through her half-opened drawers. He'd been going through her things!

How had he found her? Unless…what if it wasn't Jeffrey? Beau had said he'd missed her. Could he have gotten here in time to do this? Yes, if he'd left Friday night, after Wilder had put him in his place. But would he have done this? Cosette couldn't be sure and she hadn't been able to clearly see the attacker or his build. Beau was shorter and stockier than long and lean Jeffrey.

She headed for the kitchen. A cup of tea was in order, in the attempt to settle her nerves.

Pounding on the door sent her jumping; she yelped.

"It's me, Cosette."

She opened the door and Wilder stalked inside, a deep scowl on his face. "Whoever was here is long gone now. I've called the police."

Cosette nodded. He might be long gone now, but he wasn't going to stay gone. After leading the way to the kitchen, she reached to turn on the sink faucet, but her hand trembled and water missed the kettle and ran down her arm.

"I think it's time you come clean."

Her hands continued to shake as she carried the teapot to the stove.

Wilder's eyes softened as he took it from her, then led her to the table and into a chair. She didn't want this— this feeling of needing him. This feeling of helplessness. But part of her relished that he was here. Near her. Protecting her. It wrapped around her heart and caressed it until it was warm and pliable.

No. She closed her eyes. She would not let herself react this way to him. She couldn't.

"Cosette?" Wilder put the kettle on and then sat across from her, elbows leaning forward on the table "Did he hurt you?"

"No. I think I scared him. Interrupted him."

"Interrupted him doing what?" His voice was low and icy.

"Drawing that heart. Sifting through my things." She couldn't stop shaking.

Wilder got up from the table and pulled her up and into his powerful arms. "How long has this been going on?"

Cosette couldn't keep this a secret any longer, not from him, or from the police, who would be here any moment. How humiliating. She could kiss the equine therapy idea goodbye. Wilder would lose all faith in her. See her differently when he discovered the truth—that she wasn't the put-together professional he thought her to be. "The first time or this time?"

Wilder stiffened.

"I'm so sorry, Wilder. I should have told you when the note came. And I definitely should have said something at the graveside."

He drew back to look at her. "What happened at the cemetery?" His dark eyebrows furrowed.

She told him about the "gifts" and note. "I can resign. Leave."

He framed her face and scrunched his nose. "You're not going anywhere but back to CCM and your old apartment. Once the police are done, you can pack a few bags. Unless you have enough to get by for a while."

Of course he'd want to help her. That was his job. What he did. Protected people. But how could he trust her professional judgment any longer? She could hardly look him in the eye. "Thank you," she muttered.

The teakettle whistled.

"Have a seat. I'll get this." Wilder went to task making her a cup of chamomile tea with honey and brought it to the table. "I wish you would have told me, Cosette. I mean, this is what I do."

"I know." It was embarrassing.

"Was this Beau? It's a cowardly move, and he's a coward for sure."

"Until the class reunion, I'd say no. But now I don't know. It's doubtful."

A knock came. "Atlanta police."

Wilder let them in and shook hands with one of them. Must be a friend. He had friends all over. He took charge like always and gave them the rundown. Showed them the bedroom. "Cosette," he called. "Was anything taken from your drawers? Did you notice?"

She walked into the room, feeling intruded on by the actual intruder and now the police and Wilder combing through her private things—in her bedroom. "Nothing I can tell, except the tube of lipstick he used. He may have been about to write something when I interrupted him. I can't say for sure."

"Any idea who is doing this?" an officer asked.

She had a couple good ones.

TWO

Wilder had known something wasn't right with Cosette. How could she have kept from him the fact she had a stalker? Knowing about Meghan, who was the whole reason Covenant Crisis Management existed… It was like he was back in time, and he didn't want to go there, didn't want to think about Meghan's last night alive. Last moments. When he'd failed her miserably. His team member Beckett Marsh had been engaged to her, and in just a few hours would have been her husband, but then Parker Hill had taken her life. Beckett had blamed himself for not getting to Meghan in time, and Wilder had reassured him over the years that it wasn't Beckett's fault Meghan was dead.

It was Wilder's fault. And he'd never told a soul.

He would not let Cosette's stalker get the jump on him. Take her from him—from the team, not *him*. She wasn't his. Couldn't be.

"Do you know who might have done this, Miss La-Croix?" the officer asked.

"It's pronounced Lah-Cwah. Not Lah-Kroy like the drink," Wilder offered.

Cosette gave him the I-can-talk-for-myself look and he motioned her on with his hand. He hadn't meant to butt in and answer for her, but he was a frenzy inside and needed to harness what little control he could of the situation.

Cosette cleared her throat, her cheeks turning almost the same shade as her cherry lips. "I, um, dated a man when I worked in Washington, DC—Jeffrey Levitts. He was head of the clinic I worked at. After about six months, he became jealous and possessive. I should have seen the signs earlier on, but…" She shrugged. "I tried to break things off and he became compulsive toward me. Gifts. Jewelry. Makeup—he knew my favorite line. He'd show up at my door at all times of the night."

"Did you report any of this? Get a restraining order?"

Wilder withheld his snort. Meghan had filed one report after another and it got her nowhere. Probably didn't get Cosette anywhere, either, but at least it would be on record if it went to court.

"I didn't."

What? "Why?" he demanded.

She wouldn't look at him. That drove him nuts. The last thing he wanted was Cosette to feel too afraid to make eye contact or to feel intimidated or insecure because of him. "Look at me."

She hesitantly met his gaze.

"Were you too scared to file a report?" Wilder asked.

"I'm a trained professional. How would that look on the record?" She turned back to the officer. "He broke into my place a few times. I came home to him on my couch twice. He left of his own volition. He's a psychiatrist and far from stupid. Extremely cunning. Manipulative. He keyed my car. The list goes on. But this past weekend, I had an encounter with another man."

"Another old boyfriend?"

"Yes." She sighed and rubbed her temples. She explained what had happened at the reunion and her relationship with Beau Chauvert.

"Any other boyfriends that might be after you?" he asked, with a hint of judgment in his voice. Wilder put his arm around her. Seemed there was a whole hidden side of Cosette she'd tried to keep private. Nothing like dirty laundry being publicly aired. Wilder didn't want his aired, either.

They finished taking her statement and said she could be back inside the apartment in twelve to twenty-four hours. Well, Wilder wasn't letting her near this place alone. She was safer at CCM. With him.

"Do you have enough at your old apartment or do we need to swing by a convenience store?"

"I have enough."

Wilder led her to the car and drove her to CCM. She didn't say a single word and he didn't force her to talk. She needed to process. He understood. Sometimes silence was better than "couch sessions."

Inside, she rubbed her neck and glanced at the stairwell as if she was too exhausted to climb the winding case to the apartment she and Jody had shared for the past three years. He'd gotten used to having them both here—having Cosette here. More than he wanted to admit. More than he ought to. "You want coffee or something?"

"No," she whispered. "I think I'll just go on up."

But she didn't move.

"How about I escort you?"

She nodded.

He led her upstairs to the apartment door. She refused to meet his eyes. This wasn't the confident, feisty woman he…cared for. He raised her chin until she had no choice but to peer straight at him. "No one—*no one*, Cosette—is getting through this door but me. And anyone you personally invite in. You're safe."

"I'm sorry, Wilder. I should have told you when I interviewed for the job why I wanted it—to relocate because of Jeffrey. I knew deep down I'd be safe with you, but I was afraid if you knew the truth, you wouldn't trust my judgment. Wouldn't think I could do the work."

Her eyes turned watery and his heart thumped against his chest. She'd run to him for safety. A man she barely knew. He tucked a stray hair behind her ear. "You have yet to prove you're unable to do your job here, Cosette."

"I know the excellence you demand from your team, Wilder."

"And I know the excellence you provide. Now, no more talk about me sending you packing for making crummy choices in men." He smirked, hoping to gain a smile from her.

"I should have known better with Jeffrey. I'm a professional."

"You can't go back, Cosette. If we could…" His regrets plowed into him like a freight train.

Cosette simply nodded. Exhaustion and fear made her face seem smaller, paler. Frail.

"Has he messed with you prior to Thursday?" Wilder asked.

"After I first moved to CCM, he called repeatedly for a year."

"Why didn't you change your number?"

"I blocked him. My patients need me. Sometimes I still get calls from the ones I left behind in Washington. I don't make my address known. I got a PO box once I moved here. But if he wanted to, I suppose he could have hired someone to find me. He never showed up, so…"

"I wish you'd have told me early on. I could have done something." Yes, he'd failed before, but he wasn't going to this time.

"What, Wilder? It was 'he said, she said.' He has clout in Washington. Knows people in high places."

"So do I."

"I know, but after hearing about Meghan in the interview, I didn't want you to relive any of your past—go through that pain again."

Wilder relived it every day. Pondered what he should have done differently. He'd had zero control. Lost, and almost lost, too many people he cared about.

The image of his barely breathing sister lying across the bed came to him. Her eyes, as green as his, fading quickly...

"Who did it? Was it Parker Hill?"

She hadn't been able to speak; bruising had already begun around her neck. Couldn't even nod or blink.

Her larynx had been crushed by violent hands.

It felt like forever, but it had been only seconds before he lost her and performed CPR. An ambulance wouldn't have made it any faster, done any better.

Wilder couldn't bring her back. Couldn't make her breathe again.

She'd been under his protection since the day she was laid in his arms after she'd been born. Only three years after him.

"Wilder, this is your new baby sister. She's delicate and it's your job as the big brother to look after her. Keep her safe. You understand?" Dad had asked.

"Yessir," his three-year-old self had said, and he'd vowed right there that he'd never let any harm come to her.

If he'd arrived sooner, demanded to stay with her after she'd insisted on him and Beckett leaving... If he'd only controlled the situation better, faster, been stronger...

Wilder had wanted to kill that man, and he'd gone after him, hoping he hadn't given them the slip. That's when Beckett had arrived—same bad feeling—and found her dead, assumed he was the first to find her. He'd called the police—and an ambulance, though there was no need; it was too late.

When Wilder had returned empty-handed and seen Beckett's devastation—his blind rage—he had reined in his own temper. That much he could control. He could step up and lead, be the levelheaded one as always. Bring Meghan's killer to justice. Keep Beckett sane. Carry the grief of his family on his shoulders.

And he'd hold it together now and make sure no one—not Beau Chauvert, Jeffrey Levitts or anyone else—laid a hand on Cosette.

"Wilder?" Cosette called his name. He'd zoned out on her.

He blinked back to reality—to the woman before him with fear in her eyes.

"Don't worry about me," he told her. "I'm fine. More than fine and completely able to take care of you. I will take care of you. I promise."

"Wilder, you keep everything inside. You're not fine."

"Pot, meet kettle." He winked. "Get some sleep. I'll turn on the monitors in my office surveilling the outside perimeter. Don't worry."

He waited for her to close the door before heading downstairs to his apartment. To the piano, where he'd pound out his secrets on the keys. He'd be strong for her. For them all.

He was not weak.

But he did feel weighted down by the responsibility of seeing to everyone's safety—within his team and their clients. Like the world had been nail-gunned to his shoulders.

He sat at his baby grand and lightly ran his fingers over the keys.

He'd failed Meghan.

And another woman he'd cared about just a year before that.

But he would not fail Cosette. He'd die first.

Sleep didn't come until the wee hours of the morning for Cosette, but there was great power in concealer and contouring. She had already dressed in a gray pantsuit and pulled her hair away from her face, letting the rest hang down her back. She wouldn't let Jeffrey—or Beau—steal her life. She had patients to counsel today at the therapy clinic. These people depended on her.

How was it she had the ability to help other people fix their lives, but her own was a disaster? As she knew he would, Wilder had asked why she hadn't filed a report on Jeffrey. He'd surprised her, though, with no major reprimand and walking her up the stairs when they both knew good and well CCM was the safest place in the world. That gesture made it difficult to defend her heart around him.

But she had to remind herself that Wilder was doing his job. And it was no secret he had a tender side. She'd seen it dozens of times with his sister Caley, and with his cousin Jody, who worked for him and had been shot during an assignment a few months ago right in front of him. He hadn't left her side at the hospital… Cosette had tried to get him to talk about it—how it made him feel. He was their team leader. Alpha male. Former SEAL. The man wouldn't take defeat, failure or mistakes well. He seemed to remain in control, with a cool and calm exterior, but Cosette was concerned a storm was brewing inside him and could unleash without much warning. Her hands were tied, though. He refused to confide.

She came downstairs to chatter and the aroma of strong brewed coffee and freshly baked blueberry muffins.

Wilder sat at the head of the sixteen-seat conference table with team members Beckett Marsh, Shepherd Lightman, Evan and Jody Novak and Wheezer, who clicked away on his laptop. Beckett's wife, Aurora, held a file folder in one hand and her black plastic glasses in the other. The chatter died.

"What's going on?" Was everyone discussing her failed relationships? Her pitifulness?

"I'm going over stalking laws in Georgia," Aurora said. "Want coffee? I brought it from the shop, and assorted muffins—none have nuts."

Well, she wouldn't have to worry about dying by nut allergies. Just an obsessed stalker. Cosette darted a glance at Wilder. "I have to get to the clinic this morning. I have patients, and I'm going to see them." Not up for discussion.

Wilder had the look—he was sizing her up to see if he could win a verbal war with her. "I'll drive you."

She jingled her keys in the air. "I'm fully capable of driving myself and watching my rearview if necessary."

"Watching your rearview is always necessary. Didn't you take driver's ed?"

Humor and the twinkle in his eyes wouldn't deflect her. She didn't need him to fawn all over her. Now that she knew the danger, she would be cautious. This, sadly, was a road traveled before. "It's overkill."

"It's smart. And safe. If this Levitts guy is here—or Beau—he's watching you. Which brings me to a question."

Great.

"Now that you've had time to process, professionally, do you think it could be Beau Chauvert? He seems more like an opportunist, not a plotter. I did some checking—"

Wheezer cleared his throat. "Uh-hum."

"Wheezer did some checking." Wilder grinned. "Beau didn't show up for work the other night. He could have been in your apartment, but he doesn't have the kind of money to hop a plane or even spend the gas money to get to you."

"Unless he's fixated, and then he'll steal if necessary to get what he wants," Cosette offered. "But no. I thought about it. The earrings are expensive, dainty. Beau was never a gift-giver. Unless it was giving me something that already belonged to him. Like an old football jersey or class ring. The mind games…they're more psychological. More Jeffrey."

"Could it be someone other than Jeffrey? A newer patient who's become obsessed? Anybody giving you unwanted or even extra attention recently?"

She shook her head. "This has Jeffrey written all over it. But I'll give it more consideration and go over my patient files today to be sure I haven't missed anything." She'd missed the signs with Jeffrey. She wasn't infallible.

Wilder grabbed his phone. A knock echoed in the foyer. "Painting crew's getting an early start. Come on."

No point arguing. Wilder wouldn't let it go and she'd end up running out of arguments and be late for work.

An older man with long gray hair, two middle-aged men and a bright-eyed hotshot stood on the porch. Wilder greeted them and gave instructions. Cosette smiled and followed Wilder outside.

"Ma'am!"

Cosette turned to the tousle-headed millennial, who appeared to have rolled out of bed only minutes ago.

He grinned and held up her keys. "You dropped these."

"Oh, thanks," she said. "I didn't even hear them fall."

He approached her with some seriously practiced swagger.

"Cosette, come on," Wilder hollered from the SUV.

"Cosette…that French?" He handed her the keys, his finger brushing her palm.

"Yes." She tucked them soundly into the side pocket of her purse.

"I took two years of French back in high school." He glanced to the left, then resumed eye contact. His pupils dilated. He was attracted to her, and he was lying about French.

"That's nice. Thank you for these." She hurried to the SUV and hopped in.

Wilder raked his hand through his hair. The urge to touch it made her fingers tingle. He grunted and clicked his seat belt into place. "I only know of three—no, four—men who don't flirt with you. They all work for me."

"I dropped my keys."

"Yeah, and he tried to drop a pickup line." Wilder chuckled. "I took two years of French, too."

"Now you're both lying." She snorted and buckled up.

"Well, I know a few French things."

"Dare I ask?" She snickered and checked emails on her phone.

He wiggled his eyebrows playfully. "Double dog dare ya."

She wasn't playing into this repartee but… "If we're about to play Truth or Dare, I'd settle for truth."

"This coming from the woman who tried to hide a stalker from a security specialist."

It did seem ridiculous. She couldn't help it; she laughed. "I'm sorry."

He pulled into the clinic parking lot and Cosette's phone rang. Dad's lawyer. She declined the call.

"He's been relentless having his lawyer call. But quite frankly, there is nothing he can say that will change what he did or how I feel about him. I don't want to hear platitudes and apologies, Wilder. The day I put her in the ground, I put him there, too. Mentally." She may have written him off much earlier than that.

"What if the uptick in calls is because he's sick? You might regret not talking to him when it's too late." Wilder unclicked the seat belt for her. "You're going to be late. What time do I need to pick you up?"

She glanced at the seat belt and bristled. "I'll call you. I'm not sure." Would she regret not speaking to her dad if he died? To know his dying words? What could he possibly say to bring back Mama? To make what he did right? There was nothing.

"You want me to walk you in?" Wilder asked.

"Again, might be overkill." She hesitated. "What did the team say? When you told them?"

Wilder smirked. "We all wanna kill him. Some of us more than others."

"Let's not go that far."

He grasped her arm as she stepped from the vehicle, holding her back.

"Cosette, I'll go as far as I need to go."

She blinked back tears. "You're the best boss I've ever had." A reminder that that was all he was. Her boss. She couldn't see him as anything more. She couldn't need him for anything more than to watch over her, and she didn't like that fact.

"I'm the best boss anyone's ever had." He gave her his signature wink, but his face had fallen some.

He waited in the parking lot until she was inside, then she watched him drive away. The office smelled like antiseptic and lavender. Her heels clicked on the polished white tile as she headed for her office.

"Cosette!"

She turned and smiled. Her colleague Roger Renfrow

greeted her with a perfectly pearly-white smile, his blond hair spiked in the front. He held up a manila folder. "I found some information for you on the equine therapy. Talked to one of my friends in Michigan who runs one. Mercy Abrams. She said you can contact her anytime. Fly out there and check her place out."

Cosette took the information. "Wow, Roger, thanks so much. That's generous."

"No problem. On another note, Malcolm is here. Early and antsy."

Malcolm was twenty-four and one of the sweetest young men she knew. But he was also a pyromaniac. "Antsy, huh? You didn't happen to notice if he was carrying a lighter? Matches?"

"No, he wasn't, that I saw. Look, if you need anything else, let me know." Roger squeezed her shoulder and left her at her door.

Inside, Malcolm would be in the small waiting area painted in soft blues and greens. She opened the door and grinned. "Hi, Malcolm." She invited him into her personal office. "Have a seat," she said and unlocked her filing cabinet to retrieve his file. "How are you?"

"I'm having those thoughts again. That's why I'm early."

"Let's talk about them." She noticed an envelope propped against the picture of Mama that she kept on her desk. No writing. Her heart skittered and her hands turned clammy.

She had to concentrate on Malcolm and his disturbing thoughts about fire, but she couldn't seem to pry her eyes from the envelope.

How did it get in here? What was inside? Her neck flushed.

"...but I didn't. I didn't do it. I just did what you said,

but I wanted to, Miss LaCroix. I wanted to watch the fire dance its way through the apartment."

She gained focus. "Good, Malcolm. I'm glad to hear you didn't go through with it."

For the next thirty minutes, she worked tirelessly to concentrate on Malcolm. When he left, she stared at the envelope, gathering the courage to look inside. With shaking hands, she sliced across the top with the letter opener.

Another note.

She squeezed her eyes shut. No, she had to read it. Face this. Be brave.

The note inside read: *You work hard. Enjoy a nice night out.*

Movie tickets for an outdoor screening of *His Girl Friday* at the amphitheater and a gift card to a new Cajun restaurant. Seventy-five dollars. That was odd. She glanced around her office, which suddenly felt degrees colder. She peeped through her office window. Nothing abnormal going on, but being in here alone creeped her out. She shoved the envelope in her purse and rushed into the hall, bumping into Roger. "Hey, have you seen Crista?" Maybe someone had given it to her administrative assistant and she'd laid it on her desk.

"No, why?"

"I got a gift. Anonymous."

"What is it?" he asked.

She told him. Showed him the typed note.

"Looking for a date Saturday night?" He grinned. "Just kidding. Sort of."

Cosette shook her head at Roger's teasing and relaxed a fraction. She wasn't alone anymore. The sunshine brightened the hall, the light chasing away the darkness.

"You okay?"

Cosette smiled and breathed. "Yes. Just threw me for a loop."

"A good loop. I hear that restaurant is to die for."

She wasn't ready to die for Cajun food. Jeffrey was smart and deceptive, but he wouldn't leave her with an option to take someone else to dinner and a movie, and his note wouldn't be simple and caring, meant in a friendly way. This gift was different. She'd anonymously done nice things for coworkers and this seemed similar.

She couldn't shake the eerie notion, though, with everything else transpiring. Something felt off and sent a jolt of uneasiness through her. She glanced outside. Couldn't stop feeling eyes on her.

She rescheduled the two appointments she had left and texted Wilder to pick her up. "Thanks again for the information, Roger."

"No problem. How was Malcolm?" Since they'd both treated him, she didn't mind sharing about the earlier session.

Wilder texted back that he was on his way.

"He's using the steps we've worked on to fight the urge to burn the world down, but he seemed agitated. That was new."

They discussed Malcolm a few seconds more, until Wilder pulled under the portico. Had he been in the parking lot all this time? That was fast.

"Front-door service these days?" Roger asked, a hint of curiosity and male defeat in his voice.

"It's not like that." She held up a hand for Wilder to wait on her.

"What's it like then?"

Wilder entered the building, eyed Roger discreetly. "Ready, Cosette?" He positioned himself slightly in between her and Roger—as if her colleague was a threat.

Get. A. Grip. She needed security, she'd admit, but this behavior was unacceptable. She was her own person. What could possibly happen five feet away from the man?

He was like a tomcat spraying the area. One more reminder why she didn't need a man. Wilder should be protecting her, not marking his territory. "I am, but you could have waited in the car."

"Could've. Didn't." He smirked, ignoring her clipped tone, and extended his elbow. She ignored *that*.

"See you tomorrow, Roger." She blew past Wilder and got into the SUV.

"What's with you?" he asked, as he buckled up.

"What was with the primitive man ritual back there? You all but urinated on me."

Wilder hooted. "If only I'd been feeling the urge."

"Not funny. Wilder, let me be clear. I appreciate your thoroughness—"

"Almost thoroughness… I didn't *actually* relieve myself on your leg." His smile was smug, but disarming. He was good at that—and at getting his way. Not on this.

"But thoroughness doesn't mean having possession of me. Picking me up is one thing. Walking in and hovering over me is another, especially when I told you to wait. I'm not an object. I'm a person."

"Cosette is a human. Noted." His jaw pulsed once… twice. *Great.* But he needed to understand boundaries, and even in protecting her, there were some. There had to be—she needed them. She'd been bullied by too many men in her life and for too long.

"I'm not trying to be cold or ungrateful, Wilder…" And she definitely hadn't meant to make him mad, but this conversation was necessary and she was stressed. She sighed. "I got another 'gift' today."

* * *

Wilder whipped into a parking space and ushered Cosette inside Sufficient Grounds 2.0. The smell of coffee and cinnamon did nothing for his stomach. Had this Levitts guy gotten into her office? How? And could he even inquire? Cosette had thrown up a barrier. Put him at arm's length, where he'd been keeping her. Tables turned felt crummy.

Maybe he had sized up the dude in the bow tie who'd been falling all over her. Everyone was a suspect.

Except that wasn't true.

Something about the way they'd interacted—comfortably—sent Wilder swimming in an ocean of green. He'd reacted. Bounded in and all but staked a claim on a woman he had no right to. A woman who didn't want to be claimed. He had to respect her wishes—her boundaries. He could do that without it interfering with his duty to protect her. At least, that's what his head said. His heart was itching like it'd been dragged through a patch of poison ivy. Where was the emotional cortisone when a man needed it?

He glanced up at Amy and lifted two fingers, then pointed to Cosette. Amy nodded and went to work on their coffees. Cosette took a table away from the window. Completely out of character, but if she felt she was being watched, which was likely, then he understood her need for a barrier. Just couldn't be Wilder. She'd rather have brick and mortar.

"Can I see the contents of the envelope?" he asked. Cosette handed him the envelope and he perused them. He wasn't sure what to make of it. "What's your initial feeling about this?" Because his was screaming all kinds of bad.

Amy brought them their coffees—chicory for Cosette

and a café mocha for him. Real men didn't shy away from handcrafted drinks. They savored them. That was his story and he was sticking to it. She also placed a huge banana-nut muffin in front of Cosette.

"Just a little splurge," Amy said. "Oh, and the ice-skating with Wheezer the other night... I have bruises in so many places."

Cosette chuckled and discreetly pushed the plate with the muffin toward Wilder. Cosette had severe nut allergies but was too polite to convey the information to Amy or to stay away from the café. The coffee was too delicious. Wilder would have just said, "No can do. I could die," and sent it back. But that was Cosette. Considerate to the core.

Cosette grinned at Amy. "I'd say ice them, but that seems wrong, doesn't it?"

"It totally does." She glanced at the counter. "Duty calls." She breezed off. "I'll be by CCM tonight."

Wilder rolled his eyes. "Remember when Wheezer didn't have a girlfriend who holed up in the control room with him every waking moment she had free?" He wolfed down the muffin. "I just saved your life by eating this," he teased.

"I have an EpiPen." Cosette snorted. "And I think it's healthy for Wheezer to be involved with more than his dozen computer screens. He needs sunshine and happiness...a life outside of work."

Didn't they all?

"You asked about my initial feeling over this. At first, I thought Jeffrey had somehow gotten into my office, but it doesn't fit. Why two tickets? He'd want me all to himself."

Wilder was by no means a stalker, but he could relate to wanting Cosette all to himself. He had to push those feelings down deep. Bury them. "You think it was a legit gift? Like an act of kindness from someone who knows you might need a night out?"

"People buy dinners and coffee for others all the time. What's the verse about not letting the right hand know what the left hand is doing?" Cosette wiggled her hands. Slender fingers. No polish on her nails. She saved all that color for her lips. "I could use a night out. Maybe God is gifting me a break."

Wilder didn't think this gift was from God. Instinct said it was a threat tied with a nice little bow. "Who are you going to ask to go with you?" he asked.

She wanted space. No hovering. She could take whoever she wanted. Didn't mean he wouldn't be there watching in obscurity, standing guard. And he wouldn't tell her because it did half sound like a stalker to someone who'd been stalked before. But she had never let someone down and been responsible for the loss of their life. Cosette didn't understand that in one moment this crazy man could have her in his clutches. Wilder's gut was on fire.

He had no choice but to hover in order to stop this killer from getting to Cosette.

And what he hadn't told her, due to the stress and fear she was already enduring, was that if Jeffrey was as cunning as she said, he might be baiting her. Making her feel there was safety in this gift—that it was a coworker's random act of kindness, when in fact he was positioning Cosette exactly where he wanted her to be.

But Wilder would be there, too. By her side or in the shadows.

Cosette paused midsip. "You're not going to make that choice for me?"

"Cosette is human, remember? Wilder is not allowed to hover. I'm keeping within the boundaries."

An unladylike snort left her nostrils. "You're pacifying me. You and I both know you'll be there. In the background."

Wilder wouldn't get anything past Cosette. He rarely could and he kind of admired that. "But not hovering. You specifically said 'hover,' not lurk."

"I already feel like I'm being watched, spied on. I'd rather not add one more to the mix. How do you feel about Cary Grant?"

"Who?"

"Fabulous." She groaned and drained her coffee. "Leave it to you not to know one of the most iconic Hollywood actors in history." She pushed her cup away. "You wanna be my non-date-date?"

No. He wanted to be her date. So much for pushing down feelings. "That sounds so…mean. How about I be your escort for the night?"

"I never thought I'd have to enlist CCM's services."

Wilder never thought he'd be taking Cosette out on a date, even a non-date-date. He might have bitten off more than he could chew. But the seriousness of the situation washed over him, curdling the banana-nut muffin in his gut.

Cosette might be walking into a trap.

And the only way to catch this twisted stalker might be to let her.

THREE

Wilder tapped his pen on his desk and checked the time. Cosette should be coming down any minute. The week had been fairly quiet. No more gifts or messages, but the palpable tension rolled off her in waves and it was clear she was struggling with the fact she wouldn't be visiting her mother's grave tomorrow. Instead, the woman put on a brave front and focused on the therapy clinic, as well as her work at CCM. Though it had been pretty calm for her around these fronts—a couple threat assessments and a viewing of security tapes to get a read on an employee who might be stealing from the company.

Wilder had an uneasy feeling Levitts was biding his time, waiting for a prime opportunity to make his move. Over the years, Wilder had honed his ability to sense danger, to feel when something was off or odd. It had saved him time and again—even at a young age. All his senses were on high alert now.

He thumbed through the equine therapy information Cosette had given him, along with her proposal for building on to the stable and constructing office space, as well as a private entrance for patients. The woman was thorough. Another thing he admired about her. He pinched the bridge of his nose. He had no reason to tell her no. It was a good idea. The way she cared about people and helping them hit a deep place in him. Yet no one had been around to help *her*. Not when she was a child—when her father had been physically abusive. Wilder couldn't imagine a man putting his hands on a woman to hurt her. Couldn't imagine hurting a child. If he had a wife and children, he'd cherish them exactly as his father cherished his mother, Wilder and his sisters.

Unfortunately, marriage and children didn't have a place in Wilder's life, but he felt the cold vacuum in his heart. Lately more than usual, but that might be from the fact his cousin Jody had married recently and she and Evan were sick in love. Beckett and Aurora had a baby due, and it wouldn't be long before Caley would come to family dinner sharing the good news that she and Shep were about to have a kiddo.

Well, *CCM* was Wilder's family. He would cherish and protect them. Find fulfillment in that. He had to. He didn't have a whole heart to give. Not to any woman. Not to Cosette—so he needed to get his head in the game and tamp down the spike in his pulse at the thought of accompanying her to dinner and a movie tonight. It wasn't a date. It was work.

He needed his eyes and ears open in case Jeffrey Levitts was setting a trap. He'd had half a mind to fly to Washington, DC, and put the guy in his place, but if on the off chance it wasn't Jeffrey raining terror on Cosette, Wilder might trigger him to resume his stalking. But if Jeffrey was as intelligent and cunning as Cosette said, then it wouldn't be difficult for him to find her here in Atlanta. He could easily have hired a PI years ago like she'd said. So why now? What *was* the trigger?

Wilder checked the time again. Almost six. He swung by the control room. Wheezer sat at his desk surrounded by half a dozen monitors. "I'm leaving. You can, too, ya know. Spend Saturday night with your woman."

Wheezer grinned. "I'm seeing her tomorrow. She's

having a girls' night tonight. Apparently, they need that, like, once or twice a month." He shrugged.

Wilder nodded. "Before Meghan and Caley could drive, they'd have girls over on Friday nights once a month or so. I. Wanted. To. Die." The giggling. The whispering. The excuses to come in his room. "Don't stay too late. Set extra camera feeds up around the place. Painters will be in early in the morning, so make sure the motion detectors are off by 6:00 a.m. Apparently, they don't know the meaning of a Sabbath rest."

Wheezer muttered something about Wilder not knowing, either, but he didn't respond. Noise on the stairs drew his attention. Wilder did know how to rest, but when people were in trouble, he had a duty to protect them, and that meant even on Sundays. He'd be at church tomorrow, with Cosette and his team, like most Sundays when duty didn't call. After, Mama would make her famous roast and potatoes for everyone. Nothing tasted better than Sunday lunch at Mama's.

He rounded the corner and froze as the breath was knocked clean from his lungs.

Cosette stood on the bottom step in a dress that came to just above her knees, the same color as her cherry lips. Her hair hung in waves over her shoulders. She must have used a special lotion or something...her skin shimmered, beckoning to be touched.

Not happening.

He couldn't find his voice.

"Ready to escort me to dinner and a movie?" she asked.

He'd escort her around the world and back if she asked. "Yes, but I'm starving, so..." He splayed his hands and made light. Had to. This was too much for his heart to take.

Her heels clicked across the floor. "I hope you did

your research on Cary Grant. Last we talked, you had no clue who he was."

"Sometimes, Cosette, I like to be surprised."

"I.e., you don't care." She snickered and looped her arm in his. "And you hate surprises. You say that with every single case we work. 'No surprises. I hate surprises.'"

"Which is why I just said *sometimes*. Sometimes I like surprises." And he didn't really care about an old dead actor whose movies he'd never watch again.

Unless Cosette asked him to. Then he was terrified he'd watch every Grant movie made. Because telling Cosette no was pretty much impossible, and the reason terrified him even more.

He *wanted* to please her.

Swallowing down the lump in his throat, he guided her to the SUV and helped her inside, then drove to the new restaurant, where he insisted on a table by an exit. Conversation was as easy as blinking. The food was delicious. Spicy. Satisfying.

"I don't need a whole dessert, but that bread pudding looks divine. You want to split one, with two café au laits?" Cosette asked.

"Darlin', I thought you'd never ask." Wilder waved the server over and ordered. Cosette's phone buzzed and she glanced down, frowning. "Your dad's lawyer calling again?"

"Yes. I just can't do it, Wilder. I can't hear what he has to say. I can't talk to him or my dad."

Wilder didn't go a week without talking to his dad, but his father wasn't a drunk who'd abused his family and murdered his wife. Wilder wasn't sure if Cosette had someone she did couch sessions with and he wasn't going to bring it up. It would only circle back to him. So all he said was, "Pray about it."

"I don't need to pray about it."

"Pretty sure Paul said pray about everything," Wilder retorted.

"And do you? Pray about everything?"

He knew she'd bring this back to him. He'd kind of walked into it. "No. Do any of us?"

Bread pudding drowned in rich sauce came with their coffees. But when the server left again, Wilder felt the hairs on his arms rise. He visually swept the place. Cosette was relaxed and enjoying the night. He wanted to keep it that way. But his gut screamed a warning.

"You have to try this, Wilder. It's magnificent."

He searched for a utensil. "They didn't bring two spoons."

She carved out a giant spoonful, loaded with sauce, and held it out for him.

Something about the gesture set his insides on fire, as intense as any warning signaling danger ahead.

"It won't bite you," she teased.

He was afraid he'd already been bitten. He sampled the dessert. She was right. It was magnificent, but not nearly as magnificent as Cosette.

They shared the dessert with one spoon until she gave him the last bite. After paying the bill with the gift card, they exited the restaurant. Wilder paused.

"What is it?" Cosette asked, panic in her voice.

"Nothing to worry that pretty little head. Just precaution. Like I'd do for anyone I'm escorting." He'd never shared a dessert with one spoon with a client. His heart never jumped in his chest over clients—or his friends. What did that mean? Nothing. It could mean nothing.

Cosette scooted nearer and wrapped her arm around his, clung a little tighter than normally. "You're sure everything's okay?"

He patted her hand. "Better than." But the nagging feeling that someone was out there, lurking, wouldn't leave him.

They drove to the outdoor amphitheater and found their seats. Wilder surveyed the crowd, put his arm around Cosette, shielding her. The way she fitted next to him…it just seemed right. She leaned into him. For shelter? Or was she feeling what he was? Something absolutely forbidden.

He was guarding her well, but his heart was a different matter altogether.

The night was warm, with a half moon, and stars dotting the dark sky. A breeze blew Cosette's hair across her face. Wilder reached over and slid it behind her ear. An urge to kiss her was so strong he wasn't sure he could control it. A ripple of panic shot through him.

He would not lose control.

He reined it in. Shoved it down. Even when Cosette turned to him and peered into his eyes, and something like longing seared him.

Music played and broke the moment. Saving him from making a monstrous mistake.

He diverted his attention to the massive screen until he knew Cosette was engrossed, then he went to work…observing, listening. Waiting for whoever was in the shadows to appear and make his move.

Wilder would be ready for him.

But no one made a move. Not for the entire movie. But he was here. Wilder felt him. And Cosette must have, too. A few times she turned fidgety, glanced behind her. After the movie, they walked to the SUV in silence. Once inside and safely on the road, they talked about the film. Not that Wilder had watched much of it. But he'd kept an ear open.

They turned into the circle drive. A dark sedan was parked there, two men inside. Wilder drew his weapon. "When I get out, slide into the driver's seat and be ready to get out of here if necessary."

"And leave you to something horrible?"

He slowly opened the door. "If you don't, I'll come after you with a vengeance, Cosette LaCroix. Do what I say."

Wilder exited the SUV, weapon in hand.

The first man held up a badge. "I'm Detective Monty Chase with Atlanta PD. Mr. Flynn?"

Wilder moved closer to get a better look at the credentials. Legit. He glanced at the man stepping from the passenger side. "Yes, I'm Wilder Flynn."

"This is Detective Raymond Bodine from New Orleans Police Department. Can we come in and talk to you?"

Wilder motioned for Cosette to exit the vehicle. She strode to his side. "This is Cosette LaCroix. She works here. Come on inside. What can I help you with?"

What was a New Orleans detective doing in Atlanta? He'd let them take the lead. He punched a security code on the panel outside the door and they stepped into the foyer.

"Actually, it's good that you're here, too, Miss La-Croix," Detective Bodine said. "We were heading to your place next."

"She lives here," Wilder offered.

Bodine's eyebrow rose. "I see."

No. He didn't. "Temporarily. There's an apartment upstairs. Come. Sit." He ushered them into the conference room.

"Why is it good I'm here?" Cosette asked warily.

"When was the last time you saw Beau Chauvert?" Detective Bodine asked.

It hit Wilder. "What kind of detective are you, Detective Bodine?"

Bodine offered a tight-lipped smile, or maybe it was just pursed lips, due to the fact that he hadn't surprised them like he'd wanted. He was Homicide.

"How did he die?"

"Who said he did?"

"Don't insult me or Miss LaCroix, Detective."

Cosette raked her hand over her mouth and chin. "We saw him last Friday night. I attended my fifteenth class reunion and Mr. Flynn accompanied me."

But they already knew that. Small town. Tight-knit. Wilder's altercation was bound to have reached their ears. Wilder didn't offer any further information. Neither did Cosette. She was too smart.

Detective Bodine focused on Wilder. "Witnesses say you threatened to kill him if he came near Miss LaCroix again."

"That's not true. I never threatened to kill him. I was defending Cosette. He hauled her into the woods to do who knows what to her. She had bruises on her forearm."

Detective Bodine opened a small notepad. "Several witnesses heard you say 'Can one of you spectators come take this jerk home before he gets himself killed?' Did you not say that?"

Well, this wasn't looking good. "I did say that, but I didn't mean I'd actually kill him."

"Then why say it?"

"People say things in the heat of the moment all the time."

Cosette laid her hand on the table. "How did Beau die?"

"Blow to the back of the head. And his arm was broken. Witnesses say you threatened to break it, Mr. Flynn."

"I threatened to break his elbow, to be clear." Wilder's temper was getting the better of him.

Detective Bodine simply nodded once. "Did you threaten any other bones? Because when the assailant was done with him, he was unrecognizable. Pulverized."

Cosette winced.

"Where were you Tuesday night between 10:00 p.m. and 1:00 a.m.?"

Wilder huffed. "I was here. Asleep. Alone."

"And you, Miss LaCroix?"

"Same. Here. In my apartment alone." She sighed. "Beau was an old boyfriend, which I'm sure by now you know. He was known for being a hothead and a jerk, especially when drunk. He was drunk last Friday night." She explained what had happened and what was said. "Wilder stepped in to help me. He would never kill someone in cold blood and so violently."

"Someone was pretty ticked at Beau. I'm going to find out who."

"I hope you do," Wilder said and stood. "But you won't find him here at CCM. If you really want to find a killer, try Jeffrey Levitts." Wilder told him about the break-in and all that had transpired before and after. "But in case it's not Levitts, we don't want him to know we're looking into him. Get my drift?"

"I'll be discreet, Mr. Flynn. But maybe don't take any trips out of the country for a while."

The detectives left and Wilder locked up, then turned to Cosette. "Well, what do we make of this?"

"I don't think he's buying the Jeffrey Levitts story."

"I don't, either. But about the way Beau was murdered, what do you think?"

She folded her arms over her chest. "The manner of death denotes rage. Anyone could have those feelings concerning Beau. He was a pompous mule. Picked fights as long as I've known him. This could be coincidence or..."

"Or Jeffrey followed you to New Orleans, saw the altercation and exacted revenge on your behalf. In the name of twisted love."

Cosette licked her lips. "He'd see me as his possession, and someone else hurt that possession."

"Does Jeffrey have that kind of rage?"

"I've witnessed his wrath, but it mostly came in rants. But if he's pushed and delusional, then yes, he could have done this. And he's smart enough to frame you, Wilder. He won't like you being at my side, fighting for me... putting your arm around me. You'll be a threat. And a target."

"Did you look over your patient list like you said you would? Anyone there at all who might have developed an obsession for you? And think about places you go routinely. Cleaners. Grocery stores. Anywhere someone might see you or talk to you enough to become infatuated with you."

Cosette twisted a lock of hair around her finger. "If there is, I've missed it. And who else would know where my mom is buried, or that I visit her on Mother's Day? It has to be Jeffrey. It reeks of him."

Okay then. It was time for Wilder to take further action. He might not be able to waltz into Jeffrey Levitts's face and demand answers, but he had a friend in Washington—a PI—who wouldn't mind being discreet and getting Wilder some intel.

And if Jeffrey Levitts wanted to pick a fight with Wilder, bring it. He was more than ready.

The weekend had been hard for Cosette, especially Mother's Day. She'd spent it with the Flynn family, along with Jody and Evan, and Jody's mother and brother, Locke, who was in town briefly before storm-chasing season.

She knew Wilder had wanted to make the day as smooth as possible for her, but seeing his mom and dad and the way they loved one another, sharing playful swats in the kitchen and stealing kisses, only made her ache for family—a healthy family. She'd never seen her parents love on each other. Wilder's mom had been gracious and sweet, tending to everyone's needs. Wilder was truly blessed to have a family that close-knit.

But she'd only missed Mama even more. Missed sitting at her grave and thinking back to fond memories of her. Wilder had offered to fly her to New Orleans to visit, but she'd declined. It would take him away from his mama. Every moment with the ones you loved should be treasured and she'd had the previous weekend with Mama. That would do, but she was ever grateful for his big heart. A heart that continued to draw Cosette close. A place she didn't want to be.

Now, on Monday, it was business as usual. Cosette had seen clients and was ending the day before lunch. She grabbed her purse and the pink box of muffins she'd been given earlier by a client. She stopped at Crista's desk. "I'm about to leave, but if you need anything, let me know. I've locked up my office."

It turned out Crista had run late the morning the envelope had showed up on Cosette's desk, and she hadn't let anyone inside or seen anyone. It must have been a colleague. Maybe Dr. McMillian let someone in. She'd check with him next time she saw him. At the moment, Cosette's nerves were shot. She wasn't sleeping well.

Wilder should be here in five minutes. He'd promised not to sit in the parking lot anymore, but she didn't completely believe him. He'd also asked her to trim down her appointments, since he knew she wouldn't completely give up coming to work.

She stepped out into the hall and sat on the bench to watch for Wilder. Saturday night had been almost perfect had a stalker not been somewhere in the shadows. Not just a stalker, but a possible murderer now. What had triggered Jeffrey's new attempt to track her down? To go from fixation to cold-blooded killing? Had she gotten it wrong? Could it be someone else? No one had invaded her space. Made her feel jumpy. But then, Jeffrey had been a sweet talker. And Cosette had been needy.

Needy people tended to walk blindly.

She refused to be that person—weak and fickle when it came to men because she desperately needed love and affection from a male. She wasn't codependent any longer. That was her past. But knowing the definitions and repeating the mantras "I am independent" and "I do not need a man" hadn't changed her. She'd fallen right into Jeffrey's deceptive charm.

She wasn't going to fall for Wilder. He was her boss. Mr. Control. He couldn't help himself. It was his nature. Control his surroundings. His people. Outcomes. The man was relentless, unbending. Always got his way. And sometimes she caved to what he wanted. If she fell in love with him, she'd lose her voice. Her own identity would drown in the massive presence of Wilder Flynn.

"You're off in la-la land." Roger leaned against the wall and pointed to the pink box she held on her lap. "Whatcha got there?"

"Oh. Kariss Elroy was my last patient and she brought these to me—to everyone. You want one? Blueberry muffins." Food wasn't technically a gift, and since it was for everyone, Cosette didn't have to reject it. Unlike other personal gifts clients had offered in the past. Accepting gifts gave patients the wrong idea, could lead to transference.

"Nah. I'm trying to stay away from carbs."

Cosette chuckled. Wilder pulled under the portico, but remained inside the SUV. That was a step in the right direction, but she had a hunch it was all he could do to stay put. She waved. He lifted his chin.

"Is your car in the shop or something?" Roger asked.

She didn't want to involve her colleague. "It's not drivable at the moment, yes." Not a lie. Let Roger draw his own conclusion.

He glanced at Wilder. "Well, if he's ever busy and you need a ride…"

"Thanks." Wilder would never allow it. And that thought alone was another nail in his coffin. *Allow or not allow.* Nope. She did not answer and obey like a child or a pet. She stood, hurried outside and climbed into the car. "Thank you for not busting up on the scene."

"I get boundaries. But I'm also overzealous at times. You'll have to accept that." Wilder pulled from the lot. "What's in that box? I smell something sweet."

The man had a major sweet tooth. It was shocking he was as solid as he was. "Muffins."

A small compact car was parked in the circular drive at CCM, but no one was inside. "Do you know that car?" Cosette asked.

Wilder grimaced and cut the engine. "Yep." He escorted Cosette inside.

Aurora Marsh met them at the door. "You have company, Wilder. If you need anything, I'll be on the back porch with Beckett."

"Mr. Wilder!" A little girl with long dark curls and a glittery pink shirt shot out of the conference room and charged toward him.

Panic flashed in his eyes, but then he beamed. "Hey, Renny-girl!" He scooped her up in his arms and she planted a fat kiss on his scruffy cheek. It turned Cosette as mushy as the bread pudding from the other night. She'd never seen Wilder with a child before.

"I *drew* you a picture."

"I can't wait to see it." He lowered her and gave a tender look to the woman peeking from the conference room. Tall. Slender. Silky dark hair like the little girl. And a smile that would light up a Fourth of July party. Cosette had never seen her before.

Late twenties maybe.

"I should have called. I'm sorry." The woman strode to Wilder and hugged him, kissed his cheek.

Were they...together? Wilder kept his personal life in a locked vault.

"No, it's fine. But I'd planned to see you in two weeks." He glanced at Cosette. She studied his body language. Shifting his weight, a tick in his cheek, Adam's apple prominently bobbing... He was nervous. Uncomfortable. But not with the woman or the child.

With Cosette being there.

He didn't like this situation.

This woman had just shown up. Sidestepped his plan. He'd lost control.

"And canceled, if I remember. Pressing matter." The woman raised her eyebrows.

Was *she* the pressing matter? "I'm Cosette LaCroix." She shook the woman's hand, tired of being visible but nonexistent.

"Macy Moore."

"Macy and I are friends," Wilder said, but his voice held uncertainty.

Friends.

Cosette didn't notice a wedding band.

"I was in town to see Mama and we wanted to visit you." Macy ruffled Renny's hair. "Lunch?"

"Mr. Flynn, we're gonna take a lunch break." The young man who'd retrieved Cosette's keys stepped inside the foyer. Wesley.

Wilder raked his hand through his hair, clearly frustrated. "Sure. You don't have to let me know that."

"Right." He gave Cosette a lopsided grin. "Afternoon, Cosette. Keeping up with those keys?"

"It's Miss LaCroix," Wilder growled.

"Right," Wesley said and slid out the door.

"Overzealous?" Cosette remarked.

"Little bit." Wilder's voice was tight.

"Lunch?" Macy asked again.

Wilder pressed his hands to his brow. "Beckett's here." He looked at Cosette as if considering what to do with her. "You'll be all right for a while?"

"I'm fully capable of taking care of myself, and like you said, Beckett's here if I need anything."

"Let's go to Chuck E. Cheese, Mr. Wilder, like last time." Renny tugged on his button-down shirt.

Last time?

"If Aunt Macy says we can. She's the boss."

Since when was *anyone* the boss other than Wilder?

"I'm all for pizza," Macy said. "Nice meeting you, Cosette."

That was a dismissal if ever there was one, but since Macy was obviously Southern, she'd done it with grace as sweet as the pitcher of tea in the fridge.

"Yeah. You, too." Cosette stood in the foyer staring at the door, feeling alone and confused. Wilder hadn't left her side for a second. Not until this woman showed up with her niece. *Friends.* It shouldn't matter that Wilder had a personal life. He'd never indicated that Cosette was more than a colleague or a friend. A woman in need of help. Except sometimes it felt like maybe…maybe something was there. Something that shouldn't be.

"That's a door," Jody said with a smug smile and stood shoulder to shoulder with Cosette. "You can walk in or out of it. In case you're confused."

Cosette tossed her the stank eye, but she *was* staring at a door like an idiot. "I didn't know you were here."

"I work here. And I smelled those blueberry muffins a mile away."

She would with her condition—heightened sense of smell—but it wasn't always a blessing. Cosette had witnessed the headaches and nausea at times. "You're welcome to as many as you'd like," she said, still flustered over Wilder's behavior and the mystery woman. "Did you know that woman who was here?"

Jody's eyebrows inched up slightly.

"I'm just curious. Don't read more into it than necessary."

"Macy Moore. She lives in Augusta with her niece. Has custody of her." Jody eyed her. "Where did they go?"

"Lunch."

"Hmm…well, don't get all stirred up over it. They're just friends. Wilder dated Renny's mom off and on back when they were in high school. Then he went into the navy and she went off to school to be a photojournalist, but I think after college and in between tours they dated a little. Nothing serious."

"Where is she now? The sister?"

"She died. A year before Meghan. In Istanbul. I think she was writing a story on child sweatshops and government cover-ups. Anyway, I don't know all the details. But Wilder has kept in touch with the family."

Of a woman he'd dated some over the years but wasn't that serious about? Cosette wasn't buying it.

"Speaking of lunch, you hungry?"

"I could eat." But she'd rather know why Wilder had been so nervous and why he routinely visited the sister of a deceased old girlfriend. Her phone rang.

Unknown number.

Had her father's lawyer decided to be sneaky?

Or…

She ignored it.

It rang again.

Every nerve burned cold.

"What is it?" Jody asked, as the phone continued to ring.

"Unknown number."

"Answer it. We can get Wheezer to track it."

Cosette needed to be brave. To face this head-on. She punched the green button. "Hello," she said, with as much confidence as she could muster.

Something muffled sounded in the background. She wouldn't say Jeffrey's name and give him the delusion she'd been hoping it was him. "Hello," she said again. "I'm hanging up."

"I miss you." A whisper filtered through the line, but she could barely make it out. "Soon."

The phone went dead.

She bent at the knees, gulping air and clutching the box of muffins. Jody rubbed her back. "Deep breaths."

Cosette couldn't control the hyperventilation.

"Easy, Cosette." Jody continued to rub her back until she could get it under control.

"He said 'soon.'"

"Soon we'll put his butt in prison…or the ground. I don't mind either place." Jody reached for the cell phone.

"I'm taking this to Wheezer. Probably not enough to do a trace, but with him, who knows. Go in the kitchen and get a glass of water. Keep breathing."

A sliver of hope that Jeffrey was done terrorizing her again was lost. *God, help me. Have mercy on me.*

Cosette entered the kitchen on jellied legs.

Amy was filling a tray with glasses and lemonade. "You want a glass of—are you okay?"

She faked a smile. "Just a rough day. I'm fine. How are the ice-skating bruises?"

"Fading. Why don't you come outside and relax? I made lemonade. Nice breeze and Wheezer turned on the porch fans."

Maybe the conversation and whir of the ceiling fans would calm her frayed nerves. Take her mind off the fact a crazy man was coming for her. When he did, what did that mean? What would he do?

"What's in the box?" Amy asked.

"Muffins. From a patient."

Amy grinned. "Yum. Bring them with us. I rarely get Wheezer off those screens. If I don't hurry, I'll be enjoying the breeze with the painting crew. Not cool."

Cosette couldn't even manage a half smile, but she followed Amy outside. Her stomach twisted into a figure eight. She greeted the four painters sitting at the table.

"Where's Wheezer?" Amy asked.

"Some blonde called him inside," Wesley said.

Jody. Cosette turned to go see if he'd found anything out this fast, but Jody opened the door. "Be a minute," she said.

Amy and Cosette took empty seats. The smell of paint was strong, but the house was looking white and fresh again. The crew dived into the muffins and chugged the lemonade. Cosette couldn't bring herself to nibble on one or sip a drink.

Jeffrey was out there.

Coming for her.

Soon.

FOUR

Wilder parked behind Macy's car at CCM. Some of the painting crew, Cosette, Jody and Amy sat on the porch with lemonade. Cosette seemed preoccupied. After being at Chuck E. Cheese for an hour, he wanted nothing but peace and quiet, but there was no way that was going to happen.

Wilder strategically worked to keep Macy and Renny from CCM. They were walking billboards of Wilder's failure. Them showing up unexpected was going to draw curious minds to ask questions. Curious minds like Cosette's. She'd been staring, calculating.

"We're going to be in town for a couple of weeks. You don't mind if we come by some, do you?" Macy asked and helped Renny from the SUV.

"Yeah! I want to see the horse barn."

"We don't have horses," Wilder said. Yet. He'd made a few calls the past couple days. Found a guy who had a horse farm. Thought he'd take Cosette out there this afternoon.

But Macy had shown up.

"Is that okay? Do you have a lot going on?" Macy asked.

Yes. But Renny's eyes—her mother's eyes—held anticipation, and he couldn't tell her no.

"Sure. I'm focused on one assignment, but it rarely pulls me away from here."

Macy looked toward the porch. "The pretty brunette?"

Pretty? Cosette was much more than pretty. She was beautiful. Incredible. Inside and out. "Yes."

"She's your behavior expert, right?"

"Yes."

"You don't want to talk about her, do you?" Macy's lips twitched. "You're smitten with her."

Smitten wasn't the word he'd choose. Smitten was skin deep. Cosette was in the marrow of his bones. Coursing through him. Where were the leeches when you needed them to suck it all out? Make it go away.

"I'm her boss. I don't date colleagues. Strict policy."

Macy scowled. "Terrible policy when you're smitten. Come on, Renny. Let's go see if Nana baked cookies."

"We'll bring you some if she did, Mr. Wilder," Renny cawed. "Buy some horses so I can ride, okay?"

"We'll see, kiddo." He turned to Macy. "Tell your mama hi for me."

"I will. By the way…" she lowered her voice "…she got the check. Wilder, you don't have to send Renny money every month. Allie had life insurance."

"Y'all say that every month, but I'm going to take care of Renny. I owe Allie that." And so much more. When she was taken hostage, her family's world had been turned upside down. They'd begged her not to go, but it was who Allie was. That's why she and Wilder got along so well. They understood each other in that way. They'd been… smitten, but nothing deeper.

His team was deployed to extract her and another photographer and get them home safely.

They'd almost made it.

Wilder, it's you! I prayed it would be you they'd send. Take me home to my baby.

I will. I promise.

She'd died in his arms.

Gunshot to the head five feet from the chopper.

"Get on back now, and don't argue about the money." It was the very least he could do.

Macy sighed and rose up on her tiptoes to kiss his cheek. "You should shave and cut—" She reached out to touch his hair, but he caught her by the wrist.

"I look twelve if I shave, and no one touches the hair."

"I'm eight!" Renny hollered.

"Wilder, you could never pass as a boy." Macy winked, then corralled Renny in the car and they drove away. Wilder swiveled and caught Cosette staring. She was going to want answers.

She wasn't getting a single one.

He climbed the porch steps. "What do we have here?"

"Muffins and lemonade, in case you're blind." Cosette handed him her glass. "I'm not thirsty."

No. She was... He searched her eyes. "What's happened?"

She shook her head and stood. "Come inside and I'll fill you in."

Excusing themselves, they went into the control room.

Wheezer glanced up. "Sorry, Cosette. That phone call came from a burner. I can't trace it."

"What phone call?" Wilder demanded. He'd been gone one hour!

Cosette gave him the lowdown.

Wilder balled his fists and stormed from the room. It was time to be proactive. He called his friend in Washington. She answered on the second ring.

"Well, well. Wilder Flynn. Let me guess. You're calling in a favor."

"Hey, Teddy. You know I am." He explained the situation. "I need to know if he's still obsessed with Cosette. If he is, you'll find evidence in his home."

"You want me to do a little breaking and entering?"

"I'm just saying if you happen to get lost and discover you're in Levitts's home…keep your eyes open. Also, I need you to check and see if he's been out of town. If we make calls to his office and he finds out it was an Atlanta area code, well…not good. I don't want to give him reason to come after Cosette—if he's not already."

Teddy hooted. "I do get lost often. I'll let you know something in forty-eight hours." She hung up. Theodora VanHolt was nothing if not thorough and good at her word. He'd feel better once he had a handle on Levitts's comings and goings.

Wilder reentered the control room and shared the news.

"That's dangerous, Wilder. She could get hurt," Cosette said.

"I'm not worried about Teddy. She's not a fluffy bear. Grizzly maybe. Now…" Time to settle Cosette's nerves. "Let's you and me take a ride."

Cosette's eyes turned wary. "Where are we going?"

"You'll see." He led her onto the porch, followed by Wheezer, who sat next to Amy. She was chatting it up with the young painter flirt.

"Shouldn't you be painting or something?" Wilder asked the guy. He didn't like him lingering or the way he watched Cosette. If he hadn't come onto the property after the stalking started, Wilder might suspect him. He got a bad vibe around the dude.

"Right." He saluted and rushed down the porch steps.

Wilder grunted, then took Cosette's hand. "We're heading out," he said to Wheezer.

"Where are we going?" Cosette repeated. "I don't like surprises, either."

"You love them," Wilder retorted and grinned. He

couldn't hold it in. "I thought we'd go see a man about some horses." He waited a beat and drank in the sight.

Confusion morphed into wild excitement and then she squealed and rambled a string of French Cajun words he would never understand.

"Ahh!" She nearly leaped into his arms and squeezed his neck. Didn't matter if she choked him. He'd take it just for seeing her expression of joy. "You mean it? Horses?"

"You approve then?"

She leaned back. "I could kiss you, *mon cher*."

"Could you now?" He raised an eyebrow in hopes she actually would. "I might be inclined to let you."

She snickered, then sobered. Pushed away and broke the moment.

He'd crossed a professional line.

"It's about a forty-five minute drive. You had lunch?"

"No." Her cheeks had turned pink.

Her muffin was untouched, like her lemonade had been. The phone call had ramped up her anxiety. Stolen her appetite. He grabbed a muffin. "You can eat a snack on the way."

"Bye!" Cosette called and scrambled into the SUV.

Wilder cranked the engine.

"You're really going to approve the equine therapy?"

He'd give her anything she wanted. "I am."

"I'll see about a loan this week."

"I need to do something with that stable anyway, and extra fencing is smart. I can write it off."

"Well, I'll need one for the horses. And I want to fly out to Michigan to see a woman who does this for a living. Roger knows her."

"Roger the bow tie boy?"

Cosette ignored him.

"Sorry." Wilder just didn't like the guy. He had zero

reason other than he was close to Cosette. But she'd declared Roger nonstalker material and basically had told Wilder to get a grip. He trusted Cosette, and after discovering the truth about Jeffrey, if he questioned her about Roger she'd assume Wilder had lost faith in her professional ability. So he would give her his trust. And stay on alert. "Tear up that muffin, woman. You need to eat."

She unwrapped it and shoveled in a big bite. "Happy?" She chewed and swallowed.

"I'm gettin' there."

Another two bites and she cleared her throat. He handed her the bottle of water he'd been drinking from. "This farm is about an hour away, but everyone says..." His voice trailed off as she continued to clear her throat. Wilder glanced at her and noticed her neck had red splotches and hives sprouting; her face seemed puffy. "Cosette?"

"Wilder..." She clutched her throat. "Something's wrong. Bad wrong!" She wheezed. "Can't...breathe..."

Wilder's stomach dropped to his toes and he weaved through the cars on the interstate, ignoring the honking and ugly gestures it caused. They weren't uncommon for Atlanta traffic. "Cosette, is it a reaction to the muffin?" Obviously. He wasn't thinking clearly. He veered onto the shoulder and slammed on his brakes, put the vehicle in Park.

Her eyes watered as she gasped for oxygen.

He grabbed her purse with one hand and reached for her arm with the other. "It's okay, darlin', short easy breaths." He let go of her and dug through her bag for her EpiPen. How had she reacted to a blueberry muffin? He chucked everything out of the purse until he found it.

Fear curdled in his middle, but he worked to remain

calm. Her lips were twice their normal size and she continued to clutch her throat.

He slammed the EpiPen into her thigh. Grabbing his cell, he called an ambulance and gave their location. She shook her head, but he didn't care if the EpiPen was working. He wanted the extra medical attention.

She shook her head again.

"What? Is it not working?" Panic laced his voice. Her wheezing grew faster, more intense. Rifling through her purse again, he discovered she didn't have a second dose. "It's okay, Cosette. The ambulance will be here." He took her hands. How was it not working? "Look at me. Focus on me."

Short rapid breaths came and it was all he could do to contain himself. He was helpless. There had to be something he could do. Where was the ambulance? "Keep looking at me. You're going to be fine. I promise." He'd made promises before, but he would ensure, somehow, that Cosette would be okay.

A siren sounded in the distance.

He tucked her hair behind her ears and framed her face. If he could make the pressure in her throat go away, he would. He'd do anything for her. His heart jackhammered in his chest. "It's gonna be okay," he whispered.

The paramedics hopped out of the ambulance and wrenched open Cosette's door.

"I gave her an EpiPen and it's not working."

"We'll take it from here." A paramedic stabbed her other thigh with another EpiPen. "Sometimes it takes a second dose. What was her allergy?"

"Nuts, but that's a blueberry muffin." Wilder grabbed the pastry, wrapped it back up. How had a blueberry muffin caused this reaction? He brushed her hair off her sweaty face. "You okay, Cosette?"

Her breathing sounded more normal already and her swollen lips were shrinking. Even some of the splotches were fading. "Can you talk?" Wilder asked.

She nodded. "Yes." She touched the paramedic's hand. "Thank you."

After they were sure she was okay, and she'd turned down a hospital visit, they left.

Wilder drew her into his arms. "You scared me."

"I scared me, too. Thank you, Wilder."

For what? The one dose he gave her hadn't worked. "Where did you get those muffins?" he asked, as he slid his fingers to her wrist and checked her pulse, just to be extra sure.

"Patient. She brought them to me today."

"Where did she get them?"

"I don't know," Cosette whispered. "There wasn't a bakery name on the box. May have been a generic box purchased from a bakery store. They look homemade."

She trembled and rubbed her palms on her thighs.

"You need to find out. Does she know you have a fatal allergy?"

Cosette closed her eyes and leaned back in the car seat. "No. But I asked her if they had nuts in them and she said no. She must have accidentally cross-contaminated. Or if she did purchase them, whoever baked them did. I don't see Kariss Elroy trying to murder me with nuts."

Cosette counseled unstable mental patients. They were unpredictable. Just because she said there weren't nuts didn't mean she was telling the truth. Didn't look like she was. But maybe she didn't know and was innocent. "What's her condition?"

"You know I can't divulge that, Wilder." She grabbed his bottle of water and sipped. "But she's not homicidal, I assure you."

Well, he wasn't assured.

At least if Cosette did therapy at CCM, he could keep tabs on her patients. On her. Keep her safe. Control the circumstances, the atmosphere.

This didn't feel like coincidence. He pondered that on the drive back to CCM. No horses today.

"I want you to go rest, Cosette, and keep your phone nearby—"

"Wheezer has it."

"Then we'll get it. If you feel even the slightest bit woozy, text me and I'll be upstairs in no time. Okay?"

She nodded and he helped her out of the SUV and into the house. He walked her upstairs and into her apartment. Cosette collapsed on the couch. "I feel better, Wilder. Honest."

He ignored her and covered her up with an afghan, then brought her a bottle of water. "You want tea? I can make tea," he said. He needed to do something.

"No, I don't want tea."

He grabbed the remote. "I know you like those British shows on Netflix. Want me to turn one on?"

Cosette sighed. "Sure."

After he set up the TV, he didn't want to leave her. But he had other things to take care of. Paperwork was piling up. "I texted Jody to bring your phone up to you."

"Thanks. You can go. I'm fine."

That's what Meghan had said the night she died. "I think I'll just stick around. I like the people across the pond."

"Wilder. Overzealous. It was an accident. And I'm feeling almost a hundred percent."

Emotion swelled in his throat. "I just don't want anything to happen to you."

Cosette squeezed his hand. "It won't. I have you. I trust you to protect me."

Those were Allie's last words before she'd died.

The world tilted and Wilder had to catch his balance. He shoved the pain, the anger, the self-loathing down and forced himself to remain calm, collected and in control. "Okay, I'll go."

Jody opened the door. "I bring a phone. Ooh, I love this show! I'd stay, but I'm meeting Evan in thirty minutes at the gym. The couple that works out together stays together."

Cosette snorted "Well, I'm doomed. Actually, I'm going to take up running…never."

Jody laughed and handed Cosette the phone. "You need anything before I go? Tough break with everything else going on."

Wilder had that warning bell ringing in his ears. He wasn't sure this was a coincidence at all, but he couldn't make this piece fit into the Jeffrey Levitts puzzle. But he would eventually connect the dots.

Cosette's email notification on her computer woke her. She'd fallen asleep in season two of her favorite show. She blinked and checked the time on her cell phone: 12:21 a.m. She sipped her water, which had turned room temperature and grabbed her laptop. Might as well catch up on emails.

The laptop's light illuminated her living room, casting an eerie glow and triggering spasms through her muscles. This was CCM. A safe place. No one was getting in here, getting past Wilder.

Speaking of Wilder, he'd sent her an email. A video. She clicked on it.

She recognized the image. A pink jewelry box that played "Somewhere My Love." Mama had given her one just like that for her sixth birthday, when Cosette had wanted to be a ballerina. She still had it, sitting on her dresser in her apartment in the city. Why would Wilder be sending her a video of her childhood music box? Did he think it would be comforting?

It began to serenade in its tinkling tones as the porcelain ballerina spun slowly in a circle.

Wait.

She looked closer at the screen.

That was her jewelry box. That was her dresser. Her apartment. Wilder hadn't sent this! He wouldn't do anything like this. Feed her desserts? Yes. Break into her place and record a creepy video? No. Only one person would do this: Jeffrey. He had seen this music box. Knew it was one of the only things left Mama had given her. The sweet melody she listened to on occasion now sounded morbid.

He'd gotten back into her place, her bedroom, and filmed this.

She covered her mouth and held in the scream. Was he there, this moment? Violating her home? She would never feel safe there again.

A message popped onto the screen.

The first line was lyrics from the song playing letting her know she would be his again soon. The second his promise to be together soon, but to her, a threat.

No! She would never be his. Never be any man's again. She dropped her computer on the couch and hurried to the bathroom, her skin going from cold to hot and back. Hunching over the sink, she splashed water on her face, the drops mingling with tears.

This wouldn't end. It would never end until Jeffrey was ended.

For good.

Forever.

She sobbed and hung over the sink. *God, why me? Why now? Haven't I been through enough?*

The apartment was too dark.

Too ominous.

Every shadow was Jeffrey waiting to claim her as his own.

She wanted to jump from her skin.

She wanted to run.

Bolting from her apartment, she raced down the stairs to the one man who made her feel safe. The one man who could calm her fears. Bring peace to her heart. Settle her nerves with one look of his eyes.

She'd never been in Wilder's apartment before. She halted at the door, which was cracked open. He was listening to classical music again. It must soothe him, like spa music soothed her. She didn't recognize the piece. It was frightening and beautiful. As if two lovers had been separated forever and the memories of their time together were being replayed.

The notes raced high and low, a crescendo sending glorious chill bumps across her skin. A tidal wave of love. Of pain. And somewhere in there…hope. She could feel it all, coming through every perfect note—a major contrast to what she'd been listening to. Her knees shook.

She knocked quietly. "Wilder," she murmured. Pushing the door open, she entered the foyer and inhaled the scents. Masculine. Something spicy and sweet. It felt like a safe haven. Oddly, like home. In a way she'd never felt home before. How was that possible? Tiptoeing on, she entered a massive open living room and kitchen, but none of the decor caught her eye. Not when Wilder Flynn sat at a sleek, black, baby grand, playing each note with his own fingers.

Wilder played piano? Not just tinkered, but played masterfully.

Dazed, she watched his fingers travel furiously across the keys, bringing this story to life. She crept closer until she stood directly behind him.

This man who knew everything didn't seem to know she was here at all.

She was infringing on his privacy. His moment. But she couldn't pry herself away.

His thick hair hung over his closed eyes and the scruff on his jaw had thickened during the late-night hours. He wore a simple white T-shirt stretched over the sleek muscles of his back and arms, which moved fluidly as his fingers sped up and down the keys. Gray sweats covered his powerful legs, and he pressed the pedal with bare feet. A fresh shower scent dizzied her senses.

The melody slowed, softer…softer…until it came to a close. He remained still, breathing.

Cosette didn't dare move.

Finally, he whispered, "Come sit with me, Cosette."

"You knew I was here?" She rounded the piano bench and sat beside him.

"I've left the door open every night since you moved back in." His eyes met hers, arrested them. His husky voice wrapped around her like ribbons made of silk. "In case you were afraid to be alone. In case you needed me."

She didn't want to need him. Not for anything but CCM's security. She'd been fighting it daily. If he wouldn't open up to her professionally, he'd never open up to her personally. He was everything she thought she wanted and everything she was sure she didn't.

His expression was vulnerable. She should tell him what had brought her downstairs, but she couldn't force herself to do it. Not now. Not in this moment. This moment where the air swam thick and warm, filling all the emptiness and cold in her bones with a gentle warmth that tingled to her toes and dared her to linger, to bask in it.

This man was beautiful. Complex. Woven together like a spider's web. If she kept holding his gaze, he'd have her trapped in it. No way out. How could he do this—settle her nerves without speaking? Calm her fears with a look. But what was behind those intense green eyes? She would never know his secrets. His fears. Maybe he feared nothing. No one.

"I didn't know you played," she murmured.

"Surprise," he softly teased. Could she be wrong about him opening up? If he didn't want to reveal this intimate truth about himself, he wouldn't have been playing. Wouldn't have left his door open. Was it a metaphor? Was he ready to open up to her, and if he did, what would that do to her? Could she continue to keep the guard up around her heart? Even now it was turning to rubble.

She searched his face, hoping to find the answer. Slowly, she reached up, paused—she'd seen him stop Macy from running her hand through his hair. But he didn't move. Cosette's pulse raced as she slid his hair from his eyes. It was every bit as silky and thick as she knew it would be, starting a loop-de-loop in her belly.

He didn't reject her. Didn't seem to mind her exploring the ebony strands, and she couldn't help herself. He laid his hand on her knee, stroked it with his thumb, but said nothing.

She swallowed hard. Blinked.

"Wilder," she rasped.

He inched toward her. Stealthy. Slow. Holding her gaze captive. Not asking permission, but letting her know his intent.

She couldn't stop it.

Wouldn't.

His lips feathered against hers and parted, hovering. His spearmint breath tickled and teased her mouth. "Do you want me to kiss you, Cosette?" His nose nuzzled against hers like a wisp of wind.

Her hands trembled.

Her stomach dipped and knotted.

"Yes," she breathed.

Grasping her waist, Wilder slid her across the bench until her leg brushed his, his lips never leaving hers, but never fully touching them, either. He caressed her cheek with his hand, searched her eyes, and mixed with longing, she spotted hesitation in his.

Enough that she grasped reality. For once she was standing on her own two feet. Wasn't this her past MO when feeling lonely or afraid…running to a man? This wouldn't end with a happily-ever-after. This was all hyped up emotion on both their parts. She'd needed comfort.

Who knew what he needed? He would never say.

"Wilder?"

"Hmm…" His fingers skimmed her jawline as his mouth fully met hers, lost in this tender moment.

Cosette pulled away before it became more intimate, before she lost all reason. "This isn't right." Even if nothing had felt more right in ages. "You're emotional from playing and I'm…I'm…" *Falling into old ways.* She could kick herself. "Open up to me. Let's talk this musical score out."

In an instant, he masked the transparency and dropped his hands. Stood from the piano. "I'm sorry. I'm your boss. And that was out of line. Not right, like you said. I'm not *emotional.* I'm a good pianist. I made *you* emotional." Frustration and a hint of anger laced his words.

"Nothing wrong with emotions, Wilder. I don't understand what you're afraid of. Why you won't just talk to me professionally. Personally, even. Are we not friends?"

He licked his lips, huffed and rubbed the back of his neck. "I don't know what we are, Cosette."

That was a heavy blow. "I thought we were friends. Coworkers."

"I'm your boss. I don't date my people."

"You don't date anyone. Why? What if that beginning of a kiss had progressed? What would that have meant?" By George, she'd make him talk.

He heaved a sigh and turned his back on her, raked his hands once again through his hair, then spun around. "You came here for a reason. What was it?"

The coldness of his voice confirmed her decision to back away emotionally. He didn't get his way; now he was angry. Typical behavior of someone who felt entitled, who felt ownership over someone. If that's how he wanted to play it, okay. But she couldn't hide the disappointment and the nagging feeling that she was projecting more negative behavior onto Wilder than he was guilty of in order to protect herself. "I got an email. From you."

He frowned. "I didn't send you an email."

"I know that now. Looks like someone hacked your email address or something. It's on my laptop. Upstairs."

Where terror reigned.

And hope was lost.

"Once again, Jeffrey's been in my home."

Wilder was in her heart.

She wanted neither man in either place.

FIVE

Wilder brooded in his office. Last night had been a debacle. He'd slipped over the edge. Had lied. Granted, he had been emotional. Torn. Macy showing up with Renny had dragged up everything from the mission that had gone horribly wrong. The fact that Cosette had a stalker kept Meghan and her death front and center. And his feelings for Cosette had been unleashed in that song.

She nagged the mess out of him to open up and whined that he didn't. Well, she was wrong. He did work through his feelings. Through the piano. He emptied them all out with every note.

What was he going to do about her? What would that kiss have meant? she'd asked. That was the million-dollar question. If he allowed himself to fall headlong into Cosette, he would never recover. Never have any control. She made his head dizzy already.

But that touch last night…

She'd touched him hundreds of times.

But it never felt like that.

Like her hands were meant to slide through his hair, bringing comfort and hope. And a word he refused to bring to his tongue.

In that moment with her right next to him, needing him…his heart had reached out for her. Touching his lips, he sighed. She'd pulled away and rightly so, but he didn't expect it to power through him like a shotgun shell, buckshot spraying every artery, every muscle, shattering him.

It wasn't that he didn't want to give her everything he had.

He couldn't.

Instead, he'd let his frustration at himself spill into his words like ice. He regretted that. Needed to apologize. The email and video she'd been sent had taken precedence. After watching it, he'd called the police and met them at the apartment. Cosette didn't notice anything new missing since the last break-in except for the jewelry box. Police fingerprinted the place and took a report. It was nearly three fifteen this morning when they'd made it back to CCM.

His phone rang.

Teddy.

"What'dya got for me?" he said.

"You want the bad news or the bad news?" she asked.

"Mmm...how about the bad news?"

"That's what I thought. Jeffrey Levitts took a medical leave of absence six weeks ago. He's not scheduled to return until July."

Wilder's stomach knotted.

Teddy continued. "I used my womanly ways and found out he had surgery on his rotator cuff, but the interesting news is that he's not recuperating at home. No one has been in or out of it. I'd know because I've been watching."

"Did you happen to get disoriented and find yourself where you didn't belong?" Wilder asked.

"You know...I did." A smile coated her words. "The guy hasn't gotten over Cosette. There are framed pictures of her and the two of them together all over his place, and a section of his closet is empty, like her stuff was gone or he packed a bunch of clothing. All that hung in that little sparse section was a ladies' robe and a pair of house shoes on the floor."

Wilder's veins ran green. Cosette never said she'd had that kind of relationship with him. He grabbed his tension ball and squeezed until it hurt. "Anything else?"

"Unfortunately, no. There is no evidence of where he might be traveling or recovering. He has one social media site, but it's set to private. I can make some calls. Do more searching."

Wilder basically had all he needed. "Thanks, Teddy. I'll let you know." He hung up as his office door opened. Evan Novak entered. Wilder had given him and Wheezer the email Cosette had been sent. If anyone could trace it, it would be Wheezer and Evan—both cyber geniuses. Evan had taken down dozens of criminal cyber rings while working with the Secret Service.

"I would like to give you good news," he said.

"Why bother?" Wilder groused. "No one else is."

Evan's brow inched upward a fraction. "Remember when I was framed?"

"Five months ago? I don't have dementia, Evan." Wilder tossed his tension ball across the room. It smacked the wall and landed on the floor with a thud. "Sorry. I'm just..." What? It felt like someone had cranked a windup toy and turned it on inside him.

Evan grabbed the ball and tossed it to him. "Maybe squeeze on this and throw a baseball. But not at the wall. Which reminds me. Painters are finally on the east side of the house. Should be done day after tomorrow."

Wilder smirked. "Sorry." Guess he'd be saying that a lot in the future. "What does you being framed have to do with Cosette's email?"

"Whoever sent that bogus text to Jody used the same software to make it look like you emailed Cosette. They must have known she'd never open an anonymous email. Also, it sent a virus to the computer, which means they have access to her information and photos—or did. I handled it."

Wilder groaned. "I hate that software." Would Jeffrey Levitts know about anonymous free software that could be downloaded off the internet and used to browse dark websites and hack systems? The average American wouldn't. But if he was into dark stuff, which he probably was, then he might have found it. "Hate. It."

"Not more than me, man."

Someone had framed Evan for tipping off gun dealers about a sting he was in charge of, and then used it to put out a hit on him. He'd been on the run with Jody and both of them had nearly been killed.

"Probably not." Wilder squeezed the tension ball, then laid it on the desk. "Something else is bothering me. Muffins."

A divot formed along Evan's brow. "Muffins?"

"Blueberry." Wilder rubbed his chin. Cosette had called it an accident, and maybe it was, but his gut kept pressing him about it.

Cosette knocked and entered. Face all professional. Not a hint of warmth. He'd done that. Hurt her.

"Wilder's troubled by blueberry muffins and I have an appointment with the CEO at Mill & Dunn Manufacturing. He's beefing up security so I can't stay and help right now." Evan patted Cosette's shoulder. "But even if I could, there's no way to trace who sent the video. Sorry."

Cosette's nose twitched. "Thanks, anyway. If the CEO is wary of employee threats, call me. I can come out and go through files. Do a threat assessment for them." She turned to the door. "And can I get a ride to the clinic?"

He glanced at Wilder, uncertainty in his eyes. Yes, they'd had a little rumble. Evan turned back to Cosette. "Sure."

"*I'll* take you," Wilder said. Was she now going to try avoiding him? Not happening. He was still responsible for her safety.

Evan glanced between the two of them and landed his gaze on the tension ball. "You're gonna need a bigger ball." With that he shut the door, leaving them alone.

"Evan is capable of dropping me at the clinic."

Wilder ignored her statement and studied her. There were dark circles under her eyes. She hadn't slept last night. "I'm sorry."

"Don't be sorry. Just let someone else drive me to work." She frowned.

"Not for that. I'm sorry about last night. For the way I acted. I wasn't mad because you pulled away from a kiss. I'm relieved you did." Relieved because he could keep better control now. Stay focused. Keep his secrets buried.

"Relieved?" Pursed lips and a flash of heat in her eyes met him with full force.

"I mean…" He raked a hand through his hair, only reminding himself of when Cosette had run hers through it. "You didn't come to my apartment for that. You were frightened. I should have reacted better. Stopped playing the second I heard you come in. Let you stay the night, bunked on the couch so you could get a good night's rest."

"Let's just forget it and chalk it up to emotions running high. We're professionals. I work for you, like you said."

Another reason to keep a distance. If things went south in a romantic relationship, he'd lose the best behavioral expert he'd ever worked with. Not to mention Cosette was about to embark on a new leg of her profession with the equine therapy. How would that work if things didn't pan out between them? Questions that didn't need answering. There was no *them* and never would be.

But there had been a her and Jeffrey.

"I heard back from Teddy."

"And?"

He gave her the rundown on Jeffrey's surgery and medical leave. "She found photos of the two of you." It killed him to think about the robe and house shoes. "Did he give you back any personal belongings that you might have left over there?"

Cosette inhaled. "No...but I don't remember leaving anything there. A coffee cup maybe. Why?"

"She found your robe still hanging in the closet and your house shoes in there, too." He watched for a reaction.

He got one.

Cosette slammed her hands on his desk and leaned forward, fury in her eyes. The Cajun in her just came out like claws on a mad cat.

"What are you implying, Wilder Flynn?"

"I'm observing facts," he said quietly.

Her brown eyes were like an angry bull's. "You're jumping to conclusions. How dare you! Those aren't mine. Do you know me at all?" She spun and hauled it to the door, but he grabbed her arm.

"I *do* know you."

Her chin jutted out. "But it never crossed your mind that those items might belong to another woman."

"Not when he has pictures of you and him around his home. I wouldn't think another woman would approve. I know if we were together and you had pictures of exes, I'd have a come-apart." He tried to lighten the mood, but he missed the humorous mark.

Cosette didn't even crack a smile. "I wouldn't be so uncaring. But conversation over come-apart is key to relationships. I've had exes who operated in the latter. Too many. Too often. I'm done with that kind of relationship."

Target marked.

Locked in.

Engaged.

Hit.

She was comparing him to everyone else and he was clearly coming up just as short as they did. Wilder had been lumped into the loser pile. Maybe *she* didn't know *him*.

Grinding his jaw, he said, "I'll drive you to work."

"I'm riding with Jody. If Evan's here, Jody's here. I need to ride with her, Wilder."

Fine. She needed breathing room after last night and his accusation just now, and Wilder needed some time to lick his wounds. She'd drawn blood. "Ride with Jody," he murmured. "But before you go, you need to know that I don't think you jump into physical relationships. I just…" What? Was so jealous he blurted out the worst? Needed to know the truth even if it shouldn't have mattered? But she mattered to him. More than he could ever admit.

"Observed facts." She heaved a sigh and clutched the doorknob. "Thank you, though."

"I'll pick you up. Text me."

She nodded and left the room.

There wasn't a tension ball in the world that could absorb all his feelings.

Cosette found Jody in the CCM kitchen eating a bran muffin. "Can you take me to the clinic?"

Jody paused midbite, laid her muffin down and eyed her. "You're upset. You've been in the office with Wilder?"

"He said Jeffrey has photos of me in his house." That was as disturbing as Wilder jumping to the conclusion she'd been in a physical relationship with Jeffrey. After Wilder's glimpse of her past relationships, could she truly fault him? And while he knew she was a Christian, she hadn't talked much about or to God lately. Doing so only reminded her that Dad had been trying to reach out to her and that she should forgive him. It was easier to ignore Him than face it.

"Did he tell you that before or after you had it out with him? Your face is telling. He does things to you."

"Gets under my skin."

"It's worse lately. You're falling for him. One day, you could be my cousin."

After pulling out her compact, Cosette applied her lipstick and ran a clear sealer over it to keep the color from bleeding. Twelve-hour guarantee to hold. Jody continued to drill her with a glare. "Not happening."

"You're single. He's single. Y'all have a lot in common. Both hardheaded, always have to be right and have the last word… You both keep secrets really well…"

Cosette cocked her head and put her hands on her hips. "Thanks. I don't keep—"

"We've been friends a long time and you never confided in me about Jeffrey stalking you. I should be hurt, but I'm not. I get the need for privacy, but you never told Wilder, either. Why?"

"Fear, I guess. I've had a string of bad relationships. I've been…needy and codependent. I call my mom a textbook case. Well, I am, too. Or was. But no more. After Jeffrey, I resolved to be whole on my own. I don't need a man."

Jody sucked her top teeth. "You can be whole and need a particular man. I need Evan. But that doesn't make me weak or not whole. It makes me a woman in love."

Cosette couldn't explain it to Jody. She was strong and independent. It wasn't the same kind of need. "Every man I've ever been in a relationship with had possessive qualities. Obsessive behavior. Wilder exhibits those behaviors as well as the need for control. I can't fall into that kind of relationship again."

Jody folded her arms. "You're going to compare Wilder to crazy Jeffrey Levitts and drunk-jerk Beau Chauvert and anyone in between? To your father...?"

No. And yes.

Jody leaned against the butcher-block kitchen island. "Cosette, Wilder isn't possessive or obsessive or whatever about people. He's that way over their safety. There's a difference. You can't see it, because you've never had it. You're projecting, and the fact I can stand here and use that term says I spend way too much time with you." She grinned. "As far as not belonging to anyone, I beg to differ. Belonging to someone is safety. It means someone else has their stamp of love on you and you on them. It means they have your back. They're there for you. With you. They want what's best for you. They'd sacrifice it all for you. I belong to Evan. Evan belongs to me. It's not about possession or ownership."

Cosette swallowed the lump rising in her throat.

Pointing to her, Jody said, "And if Wilder falls in love with you, you can bank on the fact it will be just like his name. Wild. It will be fierce. Relentless." She teared up. "Like the way Jesus pursues us to make us His. You are His, Cosette. You chose Him a long time ago. He chased after you like a relentless obsession. Whether Wilder knows it or not, he's a lot like that." She wiped a tear and sniffed.

Cosette's stomach tightened. She'd never had anyone obsessed with her that it hadn't turned into destruction. "I don't want Wilder to be obsessed with me." Or God, for that matter. She just wanted to be left alone to take care of herself. To make her own choices. To be...happy.

Jody squeezed Cosette's arm. "Not everything is scary in a bad way."

"What if things go wrong between us?"

"What if they go right?"

Nothing had gone right before. She couldn't take the chance on it all going to pot now. Cosette checked her cell phone. "I'm going to be late." They walked to the car together.

"How much do I owe you for this couch session?" Cosette teased. Her phone rang. "My dad's lawyer. Again."

Jody placed her insulated cup of coffee in the holder, cranked the car engine and sped down the long driveway. Some days Cosette wondered if the woman thought she was a NASCAR driver. "I haven't been asked for my opinion, but in all fairness, you never ask me if I want yours. How bad would it be to at least answer one phone call?"

"He murdered my mother. You tell me." Cosette didn't have Jody's fairy-tale childhood.

"When I hated Evan for betraying me in the Secret Service, I hated myself, too. It was like a cancer growing inside me. I forgave him for myself. Not for him." Jody switched lanes. "We'd never be together now if I hadn't. And I'd be miserable. So would he."

It wasn't the same. Not at all. By forgiving Evan, Jody didn't betray the person she loved most. Forgiving Dad meant betraying Mama. Deep down, truth worked to wiggle free.

Fear not: for I have redeemed thee, I have called thee by thy name; thou art Mine.

The scripture ballooned in her chest. If she truly belonged to Him, she'd have to forgive her dad, and answering the phone call was the first step, which is why she'd kept ignoring them. *Lord, I just can't. Please don't make me. I want to be Yours. But I want to be my own person, too. I need that.*

The rest of the ride in morning Atlanta traffic was consumed with talk radio and less intense conversation. Jody pulled under the portico at the clinic. "I'm done being the therapist. Now to be Jody the security specialist. Evan said Wilder is mulling over those muffins. Have you mentioned to your patient what happened?"

"No." Cosette grabbed her purse. "She's fragile and if I tell her I almost died from her kind gesture, it could trigger some of her insecurity we've worked through. Now, I've said more about her than I should."

Jody handed Cosette her cell phone, from where it was lying in the console. "Is there any possible way this psycho after you could have enlisted her somehow? Even used her indirectly? The timing is weird and, like I said, Wilder is obsessive about *safety*. Which means if you don't put his unrest to bed, he's going to dig on his own. Nothing will scare that girl more than Wilder Flynn in her face." Jody gave her the you-know-it's-true look.

"I'll check into it." She'd give Kariss a call after her appointment. Cosette closed the car door and headed inside.

If she studied the same people every day or even twice a week without them noticing, she'd discover a lot about them. Their demeanor, from the way they walked to how they sat, would say much. Shy. Outgoing. Insecure. Confident. If she followed said persons and observed where they went and who they interacted with, that, too, would give her plenty of information. If she then created an opportunity to connect with them, she would be able to tell within minutes if she could manipulate them on some level.

Jeffrey had the skills to do the same. If he'd lurked outside her building, noting which patients were hers, he could gather this information. Kariss had a hard time telling someone no. If he'd handed her the box and given her some trumped up story, she would have complied. But why would Jeffrey want to kill Cosette?

She strode to her office, waved at Dr. McMillian.

"Cosette, when you get time, I want to go over a few patient files with you. No rush." He saluted her and disappeared into his office. Head of the clinic, he was a brilliant doctor, though a bit quirky. And he saluted everyone, even his patients. She'd already informed him of the situation and he'd agreed that taking on shorter days was a good decision. Best not put him off since he'd been so kind.

After leaving his office, she entered hers and dropped her purse, now stocked with a new EpiPen. Which brought back her thoughts on Jeffrey. He knew about her nut allergies. He also knew she carried an EpiPen everywhere. He may not have tried to kill her.

Punishment.

That would be in order in his mind. For rejecting him. But not from three years ago.

Wilder.

Jeffrey must have assumed she and Wilder were a couple. They'd gone to eat. To a movie. To the reunion together.

Cosette wasn't the only one in danger anymore.

Wilder was, too.

"Knock knock." Roger poked his head in her office. "Crista said you were patient-free." He entered, carrying an adorable yellow Lab.

"Is it bring-your-pet-to-work day?" Cosette asked and scratched the furry puppy's head.

"No. It's gift-a-pup-to-Cosette day. It was in a dog kennel on the steps when I came in. Card is to you." He handed it to her. That's when she noticed the red gift bow around the pup's neck.

She opened the card, a ball of nausea growing in her stomach.

To keep you company when I can't. It won't be long now. I have a special surprise for you.

She didn't want the surprise or the dog—not under these circumstances.

"Where should I put him?" Roger asked. "He looks like a Charlie. I checked. He's a male for sure."

Spots formed in front of her eyes. The room tilted.

Jeffrey had always told her she needed a dog—they should get a dog.

"Um…" She couldn't think straight. This had to stop. "Just put him back in the kennel."

Crista entered the office. "Miss LaCroix, your appointment canceled."

"Thank you." She'd call Malcolm back later and reschedule. Hopefully, he hadn't canceled to set a mall or something on fire. "Roger, can you give me a ride to Sufficient Grounds?"

"Sure. We taking the dog with us?"

She shivered. "Yeah." She couldn't just leave him here or dump him on the side of the road. But accepting him was something she couldn't do no matter how adorable he was. After following Roger to his silver Sonata, she waited while he put the dog in the back seat and opened the door for her. "Thanks."

"You sure your boyfriend won't get up in arms about me driving you somewhere? Not that I can't hold my own, but he isn't exactly average size." He nervously chuckled.

Well, of course Wilder scared every living, breathing thing with a look and his sheer size. Not that he was Mr. Universe, but he was as big as the Man of Steel.

And probably as impenetrable. "He'll be fine." Or he'd get over it. "Did you see a car or anything in the parking lot when you got here?" If she hadn't been running late due to Jody's kitchen talk this morning, she would have found the dog first. Jeffrey might have taken the opportunity to kidnap her after Jody dropped her off—or worse.

"Can't say I did. You don't know who this is from?" Roger frowned as he glanced at her.

"It didn't say on the card." Yes. She knew.

"You have no idea?" he asked.

"I might have an idea, but I'd rather keep it private."

"Cosette, is everything okay? Are you and that Terminator guy you work for having some…issues?" He turned left into the business district.

"No." Well, yes, but that was neither here nor there. "I think I have a secret admirer." She'd leave it at that.

"Well, be careful," he said, as he pulled in front of the coffee shop. "Secret admirers don't stay secret for long, and they don't like having their gifts rejected."

That was something she knew all too well.

Roger helped her with the puppy and she hurried inside alone. Guess Roger didn't want to chance it with Wilder.

Maybe Aurora would take the dog. She and Beckett lived outside the city on a good bit of land. The pound might put the poor little guy to sleep. That wasn't fair to the Lab.

"Hey, Cosette…" Amy grinned, then cocked her head when she saw the dog. "I don't think pets are allowed in here."

"I know. Is Aurora here?"

"What are you doing here? And how did you get

here?" Wilder entered the café area from the hall that led to conference rooms. Wheezer followed him.

"I have a dog."

A blank stare was his only response.

"Another unwanted gift. It was under the portico at work." The idea of Jeffrey leaving her a puppy... She fought a panic attack.

Wilder closed the distance between them and studied the dog. "He's cute. Is he chipped? Leave it to the crazy to use a dog to track you."

"He's not coming home with me." She studied the fur baby. "I don't think he's chipped."

"I can take him," Wilder said. "It's not his fault a psycho is dropping dogs at your door." He stuck his fingers inside the metal cage door and scratched the pup's ear.

"He's not coming home with you, either. I live with you. Sort of. This dog can't be anywhere near me. Wheezer? You need a dog? The pound will put him down."

"Dog shelter?" Wilder asked, as patrons scowled or smiled at the puppy, and moved past them to get in line.

"I'm at CCM more than I'm at home," Wheezer said.

"Ain't that the truth," Amy retorted, but smiled. "I can take him. Our building allows pets and I'm almost done with classes. If you change your mind, you can have him back."

"I won't want him back. Are you sure?"

Amy opened the kennel door and lifted the puppy out. "He's so stinkin' cute. What do you think, Wheezer? Should I keep him?"

"I'm down with a dog," Wheezer said and scratched the pup's ears. "Let's name him Mac after the computer."

Amy rolled her eyes. "We can discuss it later. I have

to work. I'll put him in the back room. He probably needs something to eat." She disappeared and Wheezer followed.

"Let's sit down." Wilder led Cosette to the table in the corner. No windows. "Did he leave a message?"

She showed him the card.

"Wilder, I have to tell you something. It is possible that Jeffrey could have used Kariss to deliver those muffins. He's good enough that if he wanted, he could've befriended her and had her make them. I was going to call her but this happened. The muffins might have been punishment for being with you so much."

"He might think we're together."

"We've been together a lot. Movies. Dinners. I know someone was watching us that night and you do, too." She leaned forward and clasped the top of his hand. "You're in danger. He'll see you as an obstacle. A threat. Competition. He'll try to eliminate you."

Wilder placed his free hand over hers and leaned in, as well. "*Try* is the key word here, Cosette. Don't worry about me. Now, explain why you didn't text or call me to come and get you from the clinic. Why is Mr. Bow Tie your new ride? I assume that's how you arrived. You still that mad at me?"

"Would it matter if I was?" Cosette heaved a sigh. "I trust Roger. He's a nice guy."

"You're right. Maybe. But you know how I feel about bow ties." Wilder raised a hand before she could comment. "How many more appointments do you have today?"

"One, but I think I'm going to cancel it, and if it's an emergency they have my cell number. Dr. McMillian will be fine with it, especially after I tell him about this."

Wilder scowled. "I don't think it's smart letting patients have your private number, Cosette. Can't the office forward a message and you simply return the calls?"

"Yes, but it's about trust."

Wilder opened his mouth, then clammed up. "Good idea about canceling. Jeffrey's been to the office more than I like."

"I do need to get in touch with Kariss, though. I can call her once we get back to CCM." She stood. "Ready?"

Wilder shifted uncomfortably in his chair and glanced at the entrance. "Sure. But Wheezer can give you a ride. Beckett's there."

Why couldn't Wilder drive her? Was he putting distance between them after everything that had happened in the last twenty-four hours? "Are *you* still mad?"

"Mr. Wilder!" Renny raced across the café and jumped into his lap.

Ah. He was trying to get her out before Macy Moore and her niece showed up. No wonder he'd asked what she was doing here. He hadn't planned on her wrecking his time with them. Jody said nothing was going on, but Cosette had red flags flying.

"I want hot chocolate and oatmeal cookies," Renny said.

Macy smiled and ambled their way. In fitted jeans and a flowy white top, she could be a model. "Am I early?" She looked at Cosette. "Nice to see you again."

"You, too." She pretended to look for something in her purse and pulled out a pack of gum. Spearmint. Like Wilder chewed. "I should go."

"No, stay," Macy said. "I'll buy you a coffee."

"Cosette has things to take care of. Phone calls to make," Wilder said.

He was not only trying to get rid of her, but dictating her

plans. Jody had no idea what she was talking about. "You know what? I will stay. I can make that call later. What are you having? I'll go get drinks and cookies for Renny."

"Great!" Macy said. "Skinny vanilla latte. Light foam."

Of course she drank skinny drinks. But skinny drinks tasted…skinny. Cosette excused herself and ignored Wilder's expression, a mix of panic and irritation. Nobody was going to tell her what to do.

A few moments later, she returned with a tray of coffees and cookies. She sipped her chicory brew while Wilder and Macy chatted. Macy was all breezy and fun, while Wilder's conversation felt stilted and awkward unless he was talking to Renny.

Macy's phone rang. "Excuse me."

"Jody said you and Macy went to school together," Cosette said to him.

"Macy and Caley are the same age. I was in the navy when she was in eighth grade."

"Mr. Wilder and my mama were sweethearts. Aunt Macy said so. But they didn't get married." Renny shoved half a cookie in her mouth. "When I grow up, I'm gonna marry Mr. Wilder."

Wilder nearly spewed coffee across the table.

"Well, I think that's sweet," Cosette said and winked at Renny. If she liked being married to a big bossy-pants. Who played the piano like a dream and smelled like fresh showers and spearmint, and would drive her to the brink of insanity in every way imaginable.

Wilder cleared his throat. "Allie and I were in the same class. She was a photojournalist. Freelance."

Had he loved her? Is that why he didn't date? He'd never gotten over his one true love?

Hairs on Cosette's neck prickled.

She glanced around the coffee shop.

Wilder scanned the room, obviously picking up on her fear and anxiety.

Macy returned with a sour face. "I have an issue. Mama's appointment with the cardiologist got moved up to today. Her friend who was supposed to take her isn't available and I'm in town so…"

Wilder glanced at Renny. "Leave her with me. I'm going to be around."

"You sure?"

He nodded.

Macy clasped her hands and pecked Wilder's cheek. "Renny, be good for Mr. Wilder."

"Yes, ma'am."

She rushed from the coffee shop.

Wilder grabbed his keys. "Let's go back to the house and I'll show you the stable, and maybe we'll hit the park."

"Yay!" Renny jumped up and did a victory dance. Cosette couldn't help but laugh. The sweet little thing was too much. They threw their cups away and Renny reached for their hands. "Can we get ice cream, too? Miss Cosette, will you come?"

"I love ice cream," Cosette said. Should she be anywhere near a child if Jeffrey was watching? Had he gone off the rails so much he'd hurt someone innocent? Doubtful. Would he hurt Wilder? Absolutely. "But I have some things to do."

"Oh *please*. With sugar on top. Pretty please."

Between her and Wilder, Renny ought to be safe. "Okay, I'll come."

Wilder grinned.

But as they walked toward the SUV, the reminder

that Jeffrey was out there and coming for her squashed the good feelings.

She couldn't pretend she wasn't in danger.

SIX

The last few hours had been confusing. Watching Wilder with Renny was truly something special and it messed with Cosette's emotions. Every crack and creak in the stable had sent Cosette reeling. The painters had showed Renny how they used the paint gun. Cosette and Wilder had talked a little shop about the renovations to the stable, but she was too distracted with the fact that "soon" could be tonight. In an hour. Or two weeks from now.

Wilder's phone rang and he slipped away to take the call.

"Miss Cosette, I wanna go to the park."

"When Mr. Wilder gets back, we can discuss it."

As if on cue, Wilder rounded the stable a scowl on his face. "I have to handle a small situation at the manufacturing company where Evan is point. Can you and Renny hang out inside awhile? Jody's in there and Wheezer probably has some video games."

"You said we could go to the park." Renny pouted and folded her arms over her chest. "Miss Cosette can take me, can't you?" She looked to Cosette for salvation.

Wilder's sappy expression toward Renny softened the wall Cosette had built around her heart. He clearly didn't want to let that sweet child down. But they both knew Cosette didn't need to be off at a park alone and certainly not with a child. Jeffrey might try to abduct her or maybe even both of them. It was too risky. "Well…" Wilder looked toward the house. "Miss Jody and Miss Cosette could take you together." He and Cosette shared a conversation with their eyes. He'd give Renny what she wanted and Cosette would be safe.

Yes, she'd be okay with Jody along.

An hour and a half later, Renny was swinging in the sunshine without a care in the world. Cosette couldn't say the same for herself.

"Who do you keep calling?" Jody asked.

"Kariss Elroy. My patient who gave me the blueberry muffins. But she isn't answering." Kariss sometimes got depressed and ignored her friends, but she'd always picked up when Cosette called. A tremor of panic started, but she pushed it down. Kariss might be napping, or may have left her phone in another room while she took a bath…in the middle of the day. It was possible.

Jody clapped as Renny did a cartwheel, but her eyes were constantly scanning their surroundings.

"You want to stop off at her house after we take Renny back to CCM? It's about time to go. Wilder said Macy called and she'd be back around four."

"I don't usually make house calls, but this isn't a usual situation. Yes, let's stop by." Cosette applauded Renny's continued acrobatics, then called, "It's time to head back. Your aunt Macy will be picking you up soon."

The little girl darted over. "I had fun."

"Good." Cosette had tried. Unfortunately, she didn't have the luxury Renny had.

Slipping her hand in Cosette's, Renny hummed and swung their arms together as they walked across the lot to the SUV, where they'd parked near the tree line for shade.

"When I grow up, I want to be a gymnast. Or maybe take pictures like my mom did. She was really good."

"I think both ideas are great," Cosette said, as a light blue car pulled around the corner. She guided Renny to the other side of her. It was going a bit fast for parking at a playground.

Jody paused and that raised hairs on Cosette's neck. "Cosette…"

The car sped up and came straight for her. But she had Renny's hand.

Fear shot through her veins and pounded in her ears.

The car was now almost five feet away and full-on panic set in.

"Cosette!" Jody screamed and rushed toward them, while Cosette dived with Renny into the grass beyond the curb as the car raced by.

Jody!

She turned and saw her lying on the pavement. "Jody!" she hollered. Renny was curled up in the grass, holding her knee and crying.

"It's okay, sweetheart. It's okay." But it wasn't. Cosette never should have come to the park. Jody should have brought Renny alone, no matter how much the little girl protested. Cosette never dreamed Jeffrey would try to kill an innocent child in order to get to her. How far off his rocker had he gone?

Jody grunted and jumped up, a scowl on her face as she rubbed her hip. "Everyone okay?" she asked as she hobbled toward them.

Cosette frantically nodded, her pulse still rocketing. "Was it Levitts?"

Cosette rocked Renny on her lap in the grass and smoothed the child's hair. "I didn't get a look at the driver. But who else could it be?" Wilder was going to be livid. Renny got hurt because of Cosette and Wilder was crazy about the girl. "Are you hurt?"

"Clipped my hip. I'll live. I got a partial license plate number." Jody grabbed her cell phone and punched a button. "Hey, babe, I need you to run a partial plate for me." She rattled off the number to Evan, paused, then proceeded to explain what had happened. "I'm fine…I promise…We're all fine…Love you, too."

Renny sniffed through tears. "I want Mr. Wilder!"

So did Cosette.

Cosette stayed in the back seat with Renny on the ride back to CCM. As they approached the porch, the door opened. Wilder bounded down the steps, his hair blowing in the wind. "Tell me you're okay. Both of you." He glanced down at Renny and she went to crying again.

"Somebody tried to run us over, Mr. Wilder!"

He scooped her up into his arms. "Well, Miss Cosette and Miss Jody were there to protect you."

Cosette might have kept her from being run over, but Renny was hurt and traumatized. On her account.

"I skinned my knee and it stings." She laid her head on his shoulder and hiccupped through tears.

His tone gentled as he rubbed her back. "It's okay, kiddo, don't you worry. We'll fix it up, and Miss Amy left cookies in the kitchen. Would you like a cookie for being such a brave girl?"

Cosette's tummy dipped. Did Wilder realize he'd make a fantastic father? The kind that could chase away monsters from under the bed and make a girl feel like a princess. Cosette had no idea what it was like to feel protected and safe by a dad. Hers had only inflicted fear and anger.

"I would. I think I need two cookies. I was double brave."

He chuckled and kissed her forehead, then caught Cosette's eye and held it. "What about you, darlin'? You need a cookie, too?"

"Well, I do. Thanks for asking," Jody said and rolled her eyes. "Where's Evan?"

"Right here," her husband said and swung around the corner, heading straight for her.

"I need a cookie," she repeated.

Evan raised his eyebrows. "What about something else?"

Jody grinned as he swept her into a hug and laid a kiss on her. Wilder covered Renny's eyes. "This is a place of business," he teased.

"We're totally getting down to business," Jody retorted and winked. "The business of kissing boo-boos." She patted Evan's cheek and motioned with her head toward Wilder and Cosette. "Renny, how about I clean up your knee and then you can get that cookie."

"I know firsthand that Miss Jody is a great wound fixer-upper," Evan offered.

Renny nodded and smooshed Wilder's cheeks together, looking firmly into his eyes. "Two. Cookies."

He nodded once. "I promise." He handed her off to Jody, who disappeared with her and Evan.

Wilder took Cosette's hand, rubbed the back of it with his thumb. "Now that little ears are gone, how are you really?"

She was tempted to lie. To say she was okay, they were safe, all would be well. But she didn't have it in her. Not in this moment when someone had nearly taken her life—taken Renny's! Unable to control her trembling lips, she simply shook her head. If words flowed, tears would, too.

"Ah, darlin'," Wilder breathed and drew her to his chest, wrapping his arms around her and chasing away the cold—the fear. "I'm sorry I wasn't there."

She clutched the back of his shirt and hung on to gain the strength she needed.

He giveth power to the faint; and to them that have no might He increaseth strength.

The scripture swung into her lungs like a blast of much

needed air, sharp yet tender. Entirely beaten down and exhausted, Cosette wasn't yet able to catch her breath, to renew any strength. She'd been putting on a brave front. Looking to Wilder to keep her standing firm.

But she couldn't look to him as her ultimate source.

If she asked God for strength and surrendered to letting Him in, would she also be given strength to forgive Dad?

I can do all things through Christ Who strengthens me.

She would. God would give her everything she needed—she just didn't want it. She didn't want the strength to forgive Dad because she had no desire to forgive him. Even now, knowing it was the right thing to do. An act of rebellion. Hardheadedness. Whatever term it could be called. Guilt swam in the icy pit of her stomach. And even still…she couldn't bring herself to surrender. To forgive. To let go. To give all of herself to God. She wanted to surrender to no one.

"Come on," Wilder whispered. "I'll make you some tea and you can have two cookies, too. And don't say you don't need them."

The urge to lean into him for support battled with her will to stand alone. "I can determine what I need and don't need," she said softly. Wilder had given her grace and she appreciated that. Renny had been caught in the crosshairs today. But Cosette couldn't let Wilder decide what was best for her. He might be tender at times and even sweet. But she wouldn't cave over kind gestures and comforting touches.

"All right." That's all he said as he led her to the kitchen. "Tea?"

She nodded and he busied himself putting on a kettle. What kind of man, besides an Englishman, would make a woman tea? One she wasn't going to fall for, but that didn't mean she wasn't still curious about a few things in his life. "Wilder?"

"Hmm?"

"How close were you with Allie Moore? You routinely visit her daughter and clearly have a special relationship with her family. Is Renny...?" The thought had been on her mind and she hadn't had the moxie to ask.

"Is Renny mine?" Wilder asked softly and leaned against the counter.

"A dad hasn't been mentioned. By anyone." Not even Renny.

"You think if I had a child with someone, I'd let him or her be raised by an aunt?"

It sounded horrible. "You were on tours. Who else would have raised her?"

His nostrils flared and he opened the cabinet, retrieved a mug and tossed a tea bag in it. "Is that what you really think of me?"

Throwing her own words back in her face.

"Observing facts," she murmured. In dire situations, not everyone made the right or best choice. Cosette wasn't immune. No one was. Not unbelievers. Not believers.

"Renny isn't mine, Cosette. Allie and I didn't have that kind of relationship. She married a lawyer. He was in a car accident and died right before Renny was born."

The kettle whistled and Wilder poured the steaming water into the cup, the chamomile fragrance wafting through the modern farmer's kitchen.

"What kind of relationship did you have?"

Please open up, Wilder.

He huffed, raked his hand through his hair. The telltale sign he was frustrated. "The kind that might have gone somewhere serious if our career choices hadn't separated us, but who knows?"

Wilder might have been married when Cosette had first met him. She couldn't imagine it. Not with Allie... not with any other woman. These thoughts had to stop. "You were in love with her?"

He removed the tea bag, added two heaping spoonfuls of sugar and gave Cosette the cup, their fingers brushing. "I wouldn't say we were *in* love, but we cared about each other." He shrugged. "We were kids. Then we chose careers over each other, so that says a lot, don't you think?"

"Why do you make it a point to spend time with Renny?" At first, Cosette had assumed Wilder was interested in Macy, and Renny was a side benefit. Now, after seeing him with the child, Cosette knew she was his priority, and not because he was her father.

Pawing his face, Wilder sighed and pushed himself off the counter. "When I was seventeen, me and my buddy Alan used to do some joyriding. On a Friday night in December, he wanted to go out on the ice—rarely any of that here, but that year we had a terrible ice storm. I told him I'd go, but I got hung up...in a ditch. So Alan came to pick me up. He was killed in a car accident on the way."

"I'm sorry."

Wilder let out a slow breath. "He had this ridiculous set of dice hanging from his rearview mirror. I gave him nine kinds of you-know-what about it. But after he died, I took them and hung them from my rearview mirror."

Cosette hunted for the story within a story. Wilder was famous for dancing outside of straight talk. "Where are they now?"

"In the glove box of my personal truck."

"Mr. Wilder! I'm all better and I want my cookies." Renny raced into the kitchen, breaking into the moment. Maybe Wilder had been on the cusp of revealing more. This was a step. Cosette just had to decipher the puzzle.

* * *

Wilder sat on his leather couch, feet up on the ottoman as he mindlessly surfed TV channels. Macy had taken what happened to Renny better than expected. He had her complete trust. But then, she didn't know the full story behind Allie's death. No one did. Just him. And he was taking that to the grave. Too many people relied on his protection, and if they knew what he let happen, they'd never look to him as a competent leader again.

But he'd come dangerously close to revealing the truth in its entirety to Cosette earlier in the kitchen. She'd jumped to conclusions that Renny belonged to him; he couldn't be mad for the assumption. His attachment to Renny was stronger than his attachment to the fluffy dice he couldn't let go. That would mean letting go of Alan, and it was his fault his friend was dead. Renny was his way of hanging on to Allie. Taking care of her was the next best thing he could do to make up for his mistakes in Istanbul—for not coming through for Allie. Money each month wouldn't bring her back, but it did assuage some of Wilder's guilt.

That tragic night had replayed in his head thousands of times, and each time he'd done something different to save her. She hadn't died in his arms. Meghan's death had replayed, too. Was having Beckett work for him part of his way of hanging on to Meghan? Wilder sipped his sweet tea and pondered that. No. Beckett wasn't his dice in the glove box or his human connection.

CCM was his connection to Meghan. He called it a memorial, and while that was true, it was so much more than that. Cosette might call it unhealthy. Obsessive. Like keeping these people as possessions that he couldn't part with. But how did one let go of a loved one? Was it any different than Cosette visiting her mother's grave with flowers every single Mother's Day? Like trying to relive one last day with her?

He couldn't give up these connections. Couldn't move forward. He was stuck in regret. Stuck replaying the tragedies with better outcomes, where everyone lived. Everyone was happy. No one was scarred.

What he wouldn't give right now to have someone to lean on. To confide in. But there was no one. He was the top of the tier. The leader. The strength of his team. His family.

Questions would have to remain unanswered.

Questions like how to let go. How to move on. How to fight fear when you were supposed to be fearless. How to admit weakness when you were supposed to be strong. How to admit failure when you were supposed to always succeed.

He hadn't succeeded in finding Jeffrey Levitts. But then he hadn't given the signal to hack into his financials and track him. He had to play this by the book, so when it came time to put this creep away, nothing would be inadmissible in court. Aurora had made the boundaries clear. The woman was an astute attorney and had immersed herself in Georgia law since moving here and marrying Beck.

Beck had moved on. He was happy and building a life with Aurora on a farm with chickens. A baby was coming soon for them. Wilder didn't hold it against him. Had never expected him to pine over Meghan forever.

A quiet knock sounded on his door. He checked the time: after 9:00 p.m. He raised himself off the couch with a grunt. Wilder's knees were beginning to protest how hard he had worked them. He opened the door.

Cosette stood before him. She'd changed into jeans

and an oversize T-shirt. Her hair was plopped in a mess on her head, revealing a slender neck.

"Everything okay?" he asked, and invited her inside with a sweep of his arm.

She glanced into the room, hesitated. He wouldn't try to kiss her again. Wouldn't lose control. But those lips coated in cherry red teased him. Did this woman's lipstick never come off? "I'm not sure. I was planning on going by Kariss Elroy's place with Jody this afternoon, but then we were nearly run down. I've called a few times this evening and I'm still getting voice mail. That worries me."

Cosette's concern for everyone touched Wilder in deep places. She paused at the piano, ran a hand along the sleek edge, then turned.

"Would you like to go by there?" he asked.

The uncertainty and fear in her eyes had him itching to pull her close, but she wanted a professional protector— even if they were friends—and lines couldn't be crossed again. She'd pulled away from a kiss. Cosette thought he was a hovering bonehead like the others she'd fallen for in the past. Men who had destroyed her. No amount of higher education was going to pull that pain away and blast the iron around her heart.

"Not every man will fail you, Cosette." The statement rushed out before he could contain it.

She half smiled. "I'm not prepared to take those chances. I'm happy on my own."

"Are you?"

"Yes. I like belonging to myself." Doubt laced her words. "I make the calls in my life. I decide what I want and when I want it. I answer to no one." She lifted her chin.

His laugh was humorless. "You make it sound like

a relationship has to be about a man being in charge of the woman."

"It doesn't have to be. I know that. But I seem to…"

"Seem to what?"

She closed her eyes and sighed. "Fall for the wrong men."

"Men like me?" Cosette had compared him to all the other wrong men in her life. It still rankled.

"I'm not falling for you," she said with force.

He wasn't implying *that,* and started to say so, but she didn't give him a chance.

"But if I'm being honest, yes."

That stirred up his dander. "You think I'd stalk you? Terrorize you? *Manhandle* you?" What was this woman thinking?

She glanced away, then met his eyes. "No, but you're controlling, obsessive and intrusive."

He opened his mouth to argue, but was stunned speechless. He clamped his lips together and silently counted to ten. "Well, I guess it's a good thing you're not falling for me then, isn't it?" Wilder tried to control his clipped tone, but it edged out.

She smoothed invisible wrinkles on her sleeve. "I guess so. Besides, even if I were, you don't date employees."

"Or mouthy, opinionated, pushy women. You fall under all three of those."

"I'm…" She blew out a heavy breath, reeling in the fire in her eyes. Yeah, it stung to hear false accusations. Though she was all those things, but he never saw them as weaknesses. He admired and respected every one of those attributes. Flat out enjoyed them at times.

"Drive me to Kariss's?"

Conversation over. It was going nowhere fast, anyway. He slipped his shoes on and grabbed his keys, wallet and

gun. The ride to Kariss's small home in a shoddy neighborhood was relatively quiet.

The Craftsman house had peeling paint and overgrown
bushes out front. Darkness permeated the inside. In a
burst, Wilder felt the hairs on his arms raise. "I don't
like this."

Cosette clutched her purse. "I don't, either."

He exited the SUV, gun drawn. "Stay right behind
me." He ought to leave her in the car, but if someone was
lurking, the minute Wilder disappeared into the house,
Cosette would be at risk. He couldn't imagine coming
out to find her missing. Sidling up behind him, Cosette
briefly touched his upper arm.

Wilder crept to the front door. Knocked lightly. Turned
the knob.

It was locked. The blinds had been drawn. He paused.
Listened.

Frogs croaked.

Cosette's breathing was shaky.

Leaves rustled in the trees, but no sound came from
inside. Not even a TV. It wasn't that late.

"Let's go around back." Wilder unlatched the metal
lock on the chain-link fence and surveyed the small backyard. "Okay," he whispered and headed for the rear entrance. The hinges screeched as he opened the screen door,
before testing the wooden one. "Unlocked. Stay behind
me." He'd shelter her if anything inside was hazardous.

He stepped into a kitchen smelling of Mexican spices.
Dinner dishes had been left on the counter. Tacos. Ice
dropped into the holder in the freezer with clinks and
clanks. Otherwise, the place was silent.

No. There was a sound.

Cosette must have heard it, too. She clutched his bi-
ceps. "Wilder."

Grasping the knob on the door that led to the one-car garage, Wilder flung it open. Fumes racked his senses and he covered his nose.

Kariss's car was running.

"Oh, Wilder," Cosette whispered frantically through her shirt, which she was using as a mask.

Feeling along the wall, he found the garage door button and punched it. The familiar squeal of it opening sounded and the automatic light kicked on.

Bounding down the steps, Wilder yanked open the driver's door.

Kariss Elroy's head rested back against the seat as if she was sleeping, but Wilder knew better even before he checked for a pulse.

"Wilder, is she…" Cosette's voice shook.

He turned off the engine. "Call the police." He started CPR, knowing it was a lost cause, but he had to do something. Cosette gave the dispatcher the information and called for an ambulance.

Wilder glanced up and met her eyes.

Cosette was studying the car, her lips trembling and her eyes as wide as saucers. "What's the matter?"

"Wilder. This is the car that ran us down earlier."

Wilder held a lifeless Kariss Elroy in his arms. "Are you sure?"

"I'm positive." She covered her mouth, pain etching her lovely facial features. Tears pooled in her eyes and she shook her head. This entire situation was confusing, frightful and seemingly endless. People she cared about were dying, and judging by the paleness in her cheeks, and her shaking shoulders, Cosette was expecting her own outcome to be the same as Kariss Elroy's. Wilder gently laid Kariss back against the seat as the ambulance sirens let them know they were close.

He closed the distance between them and drew Cosette against his chest. "It's going to be okay. There was nothing you could do." He stroked her hair.

She shook her head. "I could have checked on her earlier. I could have… I don't know. Why would she run me down? Did Jeffrey convince her, somehow, and then guilt drove her to this? I don't understand."

Wilder didn't have all the pieces, either. "Did you see if the driver was male or female? Jeffrey could have 'borrowed' her car, or stolen it and framed Kariss, then silenced her to keep her from talking."

Cosette peered into his eyes. "You think this was a homicide?"

"I don't know." Nothing was adding up, but his stomach twisted in tight knots. Things were going to escalate even further. He had to stop it.

The ambulance and police arrived.

Officers questioned them. Cosette explained why they had come to Kariss's.

"Did you report the almost hit-and-run?" an officer asked.

They should have, but it was easier to have Wheezer pull the partial plate number. Wilder spoke. "No. I'm officially investigating the case. It's documented in my notes."

The officer raised an eyebrow and scribbled on his notepad, then took their personal information for follow-up questions.

"Can you get a forensics team out here to take a look? It's possible this isn't a suicide," Wilder offered. If the guy wouldn't acquiesce, he'd call in a favor from a friend at the Atlanta PD.

"We'll make a note."

And Wilder would make a call.

When the questions were over, Wilder led Cosette to the SUV. "What would Jeffrey have to gain by using your patient to bring you muffins and then killing her—if he did?"

Cosette rubbed her hands on her thighs and shivered. He cranked up the heat, knowing she was shaking from fear, but maybe the added warmth would help. He hated seeing her this frightened and unsure.

"Jeffrey is calculating. Arrogant. He might have used Kariss just to see if he could. To torture me. Because this is torture, Wilder. Kariss was fragile. And she's dead because of me, and he's coming... He's going to kill me," she squeaked. "He's gone off the deep end. I knew it for sure when he was willing to take out an innocent child. There's no one he won't kill to make me his. Wilder... you should send me away. To a safe house or something."

Wilder gritted his teeth. This man had terrorized Cosette long enough. He grabbed her hand as they pulled into the circle drive at CCM. He squeezed it and waited for her to make eye contact. "I will not let him get his hands on you."

"He's cunning."

What was it going to take to make her understand that Wilder would die in order to keep her safe? He had to calm her fears and doubts about his abilities—and revealing the truth about Allie and Meghan wouldn't do that. He regretted now, on some level, confiding in her about Alan. "Cosette, I don't care how cunning he is. I will protect you. Please believe me."

"I do." She wiped a tear from her cheek. "But I'm losing my mind. I'm in a constant state of fear and I'm trying hard to be brave, but I'm wearing thin. He's around every corner. He's every shadow. Every creak and pop. He's murdering people I—I care about. I don't know how much more I can take before he breaks me."

Wilder framed her face, wishing there was more he could do. Maybe there was. "Do you want to sleep at my place tonight? I can take the couch."

Her teary eyes had washed some eyeliner down her cheeks, but that cherry red lipstick stayed strong. It was a sight to behold—beautiful and pitiful at the same time. "You don't mind?" she asked.

"No." Whatever she needed to feel safe.

He led her into his apartment and locked the door behind them. "You'll be safe here. Not that you wouldn't be upstairs, too..."

"Upstairs feels pretty far away." Cosette slipped off her shoes.

Being near him made her feel safe. Good. "Do you want to go get pajamas or something? I can walk you up. Wait for you."

She half smiled. "Thank you, but no. I'm exhausted. I can't believe Kariss is dead. I didn't see any suicidal signs, Wilder. She's struggled with them in the past, but her therapy was going well. She was healing. Making strides toward a new and better life. Which is why I know she was murdered. What if the police rule it a suicide?"

"I'll stay on top of it. We'll find the truth and bring her killer to justice."

He led her into his bedroom, switched on the lamp at the dresser by the door. "I'm only a few feet away. You can sleep peacefully. If you need me..."

She slowly surveyed his bedroom, then turned to him. "Thank you." Her voice was thick with emotion. "For keeping me safe. For giving up your bed."

He tucked a lock of hair behind her ear. "Good night," he whispered and shut the door behind him. He padded to the linen closet in the bathroom and grabbed a blanket and extra pillow. Tossing them on the couch, he sighed and collapsed.

Cosette LaCroix was ten feet away, in his home.

But only for protection. That wasn't exactly how he'd pictured it. He couldn't afford to imagine her as his wife. But lately, the thoughts had come more often. Sharing a home. A family. Even a dog.

Tomorrow, he'd strip off the sheets and wash away her sweet scent. No point enduring torture if he didn't have to.

Sleep wasn't going to come. One hour ticked into two, into three. He tossed off the blanket and tiptoed to his bedroom. Cracking open the door, he peeked in on Cosette.

The soft glow of light coming from the bathroom illuminated her form. She was swaddled in his thick brown-and-blue comforter, her hair fanned across his pillow. Quietly, he closed the door.

He needed fresh air. Needed to escape this scene and she didn't look like she'd be waking up soon. She'd never know he was gone, and he'd be back before she woke.

He set the alarm using his phone. If anything was off it would alert him, and he slipped from the house. He paced the porch and wandered out to the stable. Before long, Cosette's mark would be on this property more than his own. Her offices. Her private road. Chances were she'd move back into her old apartment upstairs for good, to be closer to patients and the office.

And every day Wilder would have to watch the life he longed for but couldn't have slip away.

Hay rustled. Wilder turned, but something smacked him upside the head, leaving him in darkness.

SEVEN

Cosette awoke disoriented, the clean scent of soap and something distinctly masculine muddying her thoughts. She blinked as she adjusted to the darkness.

Cottony sheets. A fluffy comforter. Walnut furniture.

She was in Wilder's bed. Raising up, she glanced at his clock. He still used an alarm clock? It was nearly 2:00 a.m. She'd slept hard and deep for almost four hours. Pulling the covers up around her, she inhaled deeply and her pulse spiked. Mercy, they smelled good. Like Wilder, minus the signature scent of spearmint from the gum he chewed, like a smoker trying to quit.

She could get lost in this giant bed. The downy comforter. Fluffy pillows. She could imagine sleeping late. Eating breakfast and sipping coffee here.

But the reality was this wasn't her bed. Would never be. And Kariss Elroy was dead. Jeffrey Levitts might have killed her. He'd probably killed Beau Chauvert.

A burst of color caught her eye from the window across the room. Slipping out of bed, she hurried to it, squinted into the night.

Heart lurching into her throat, she screamed for Wilder.

The stable was on fire.

"Wilder!" She raced into the living room. The couch was empty. Nothing but a pillow and blanket. Where was he? She continued screaming for him and dashing through the apartment while she dialed 911 for the fire department.

Exiting his apartment, she tried the control room. TV monitors showed the property, including the stable. Faint, almost undetectable, it appeared there was someone in the stable. Ice settled in the pit of her stomach and she flew barefoot out the door, down the porch stairs and across the yard toward the flames, the alarm she'd set off screeching.

She squinted due to the brilliance of the flames on the back walls and licking up the roof. Inside the stable, Wilder lay facedown. No time to waste or wait for the fire department. He might already be dead from injuries or smoke inhalation.

Smoke billowed from the building. Cosette covered her mouth and nose with her T-shirt and swallowed down fear. Wilder was in trouble. Hunching her shoulders, she entered the burning stable, the heat searing her skin, breaking her out in a sweat.

Four of the back stalls were ablaze. It wouldn't be long before the entire place was ash. "Wilder!" She coughed, eyes burning. Making her way to him, she grunted as she rolled his massive frame over. A trickle of blood ran down his temple, but he was breathing. Barely.

Her heart raced at a frantic speed. She couldn't let him die, but she couldn't lift well over two hundred pounds of muscle on a six-foot-three frame. Grabbing his arms, she used all her might and pulled.

God, help me get him out of here. Give me strength. Hopefully, He'd show her—and Wilder—mercy. She wasn't doing much of what God asked lately.

Struggling, she dragged Wilder a few inches, her muscles pulling taut and shaking from exertion.

Must. Get. Him. Out.

She felt a muscle pull in her back and she cried out. Sweat dripped down her cheeks.

Crackling and popping came from above, then hissing. Hot bits of ash burned her bare arms as they fell from the ceiling.

At this rate, she'd never get him out. She regrouped and tightened her grip under his arms, his head falling back. Terror shot acid into her throat.

Wood splintering caught her attention. The beam above was giving way. If it fell, Wilder would be crushed.

She coughed and gripped harder, ignoring the pain in her back. Cosette yanked with everything she had and dragged him a foot farther toward the stable doors and freedom.

The heat was too intense. Her throat burned, her tongue as dry as winter grass.

One more heave. That's all she needed.

The beam overhead sounded like a lion's roar as it finally broke.

Ashes fell. Embers.

Her heart lurched into her throat with the adrenaline and she pulled with every fiber of her being.

The beam crashed to the stable floor, erupting in flames only inches from where Wilder had been. With no time for shock, she hauled him through the open doors and a few feet away.

Thank You, Lord.

The fire truck siren blared.

She collapsed next to him. "Wilder." She patted his cheeks, which were black with soot. His hair was wet and matted to his forehead. "Wake up!"

He didn't move, but she saw his chest faintly rise and fall. "Please wake up!"

Suddenly, he jolted up, coughing and beating his chest.

Relief flooded her. "You're alive," she said and threw herself against him while he coughed into her hair.

First responders rushed up and attended to Wilder.

"Ma'am," a young paramedic said, "you have a burn on your arm."

She glanced down at her forearm, where an ember had singed her skin. Red. Blistered. "Yes, I guess I do." Now that he mentioned it, the pain throbbed.

He cleaned and bandaged the wound.

The firefighters doused the flames, but it was too late for the stable. It was gone, leaving nothing but smoke and ash.

Wilder growled and knocked the oxygen mask away. "I'm fine." A deep scowl lined his filthy brow. Eyes smoldering, he stood and watched the stable.

Cosette stood beside him. "They're only doing their jobs. You inhaled a lot of smoke. And you have a head injury."

"I've had worse," he groused.

"It's just a stable, Wilder." She laid a hand on his arm, but he wrenched it away.

"I don't care about this stupid stable!"

Cosette flinched at his tone, his volume.

He pointed at her arm. "You're hurt. Because of me." He stalked toward the arriving police car.

If he didn't care about the stable, then why had he come out here alone to try and save it? Unless… She rushed to the police car, where Wilder was speaking with an officer. "…he got me before I could do anything."

He hadn't come out to save the burning stable. He'd been attacked. On his own property! She'd warned him this would happen. That Jeffrey would try to kill him.

"You came out here and heard something." The officer diligently wrote on his notepad. "You turned and someone whacked you, then set the barn on fire?"

"Correct."

"Why did you come out so late?"

Wilder stepped closer and the policeman shifted backward. Leave it to Wilder to intimidate even an officer of the law. "I can go anywhere on my property at any hour. The question you need to be asking is who was dumb enough to be out here, knowing I have security. It's a *security* company." As if a light bulb had flicked on, Wilder strode toward the house.

"Wait!" Cosette called and chased after him.

She reached him at the front door. "Wilder, did you see who attacked you? Was it Jeffrey?"

He ignored her, stormed into the control room and disarmed the squealing alarm. Searching the feed, he watched as a figure skulked around the stable.

Cosette shook her head. "That's not Jeffrey."

"No, it's not."

It was the older guy from the painting crew. His face was hidden, but the ball cap was unmistakable. He always wore it. Why would he want to hurt Wilder? He couldn't know that Wilder would be in the stable this time of night. "You must have surprised him working to set the fire."

Wilder nodded.

"Why would the painter—"

"Frank. Frank Steadham."

"Why would Frank want to burn down the stable? It's not like you asked him to paint it."

Wilder turned, raised an eyebrow and smirked.

Cosette wasn't sure where the snark had come from. A release, maybe, from the enormous amount of fear earlier.

"I'm not sure he did. He's been on-site enough to know we have state-of-the-art security. So if he was going to burn it to the ground, why wear the hat he wears constantly and painter's clothing?"

Good point. "You think someone is framing him? Someone like Jeffrey?"

Wilder rubbed the stubble on his chin. "Possibly." He snagged his cell phone and hit a button. "Wheezer, I need you to come in and work on some imaging from tonight's footage." He gave him the lowdown and clicked off. "We need to see if we can't get a solid ID on Frank. Either he's a moron, he was put up to it for a lot of cash, or it wasn't him."

"If you can't get a clear picture of his face, then what?" Cosette asked.

"When I talk to him, you'll be studying his behavior. You'll know."

Would she? She'd failed before.

The lieutenant entered the control room. "Mr. Flynn, the fire is out but we couldn't salvage any of it. It appears the blaze was started in the northwest corner. Doused in gasoline. Police found an empty gas can in the woods. Took it as evidence."

Wilder nodded. "Thank you. And thank you for dragging me out of there. I owe you."

The lieutenant pointed at Cosette. "You owe her. She pulled you out before we arrived."

Cosette's neck and cheeks heated.

"I'll get a copy of my report to you." He grinned at Cosette. "Ma'am."

When he left, Wilder spun on her. "That stable was kindling. You ran into it for me? That's how you got that injury!"

"Of course I did."

"Are you *mad*, woman?" Wilder raked a hand through his hair.

Cosette's temper flared. "You think I was just gonna stand there and watch you burn? Are *you* mad?" She stepped into his personal space. "You're going to jump on my case over the fact you're alive? You have some nerve!"

"You should have gone straight to the panic room and called one of the team when you saw the fire—and stayed there until it was safe. What if Jeffrey had abducted you? Hurt you? Thrown you in the fire with me?" His voice boomed, hot and furious.

"Then we'd have burned together, you big, stupid... *man*!" As if she was going to cower while the fire ate him alive.

Wilder loomed over her, his voice low and menacing. "Did you just call me stupid?"

She squared her shoulders, temper out of control. "Yeah. I'm mouthy and opinionated, remember?"

His cheek pulsed. "*I'm* stupid? I didn't run into a burning barn and attempt to drag a grown man outside. You could have died."

"I didn't attempt it. I *did* it. And I'd...I'd do it again. I'd do it a hundred times," she hollered. How could he want her to leave him there to die? Was he that prideful? Her head was on fire and ready to explode; tears betrayed her and her back ached something fierce. "You don't know what it was like to run out there and see the strongest, bravest man I've ever known lying so still...so helpless, with flames licking up the walls, about to consume him. You don't know the terror. But you'd rather die than have a woman rescue you. Have a chunk of your pride cut out."

"That's what you think this is about?" His eyes narrowed. "Pride? Cosette, I have a woman on my team! I put my life in her hands often. This isn't a battle of the sexes. Now who doesn't know who?"

"I'm on your team, too! Would you be acting like a horse's behind if it had been Jody?"

"No! But you're not Jody!"

No. Cosette was helpless. Defenseless. All the things she didn't want to be anymore, but all the things Wilder saw in her.

Wilder's anger was bubbling over and spilling onto Cosette. He wasn't mad at her. Well, he was. The thought of her dying in a fire trying to save him, or being abducted, scared him more than anything. Her life was more important than his. He was supposed to be protecting her, not being blindsided and lit on fire. This could have turned out much differently.

Cosette was right, though. She hadn't died or been kidnapped, but she had been burned. She had saved his life. Risked everything to keep him safe. Emotions from the deepest part of him rose.

"Well, you're welcome anyway! You ungrateful jerk. I changed my mind. Next time, I might leave you!" She stormed toward the door, but he grabbed her uninjured arm and yanked her against him.

Let every fleeting thought but Cosette leave his mind as he descended on her lips.

She gasped, then met his thirst as if she were as parched as he was, as if they'd rehearsed this duet a million times.

They played it grandioso. Harmony perfected.

Raw. Uncontrollable.

She was the fire, burning, consuming, ravaging every part of him. Her hands slid into the hair at the base of his neck and he gripped her waist tighter.

How would he ever get this woman out of his very marrow? Everything about her moved him. Her love of people and her calling to care for them. Her brilliant mind. Keen sense. Her independence and bravery. And the French Cajun spice that was all Cosette. She didn't back down. Didn't cower. This woman was a force.

Wilder had begun with the crescendo. That's not how he wanted to kiss her. Well, it was…but she deserved a buildup. He slowed the tempo, released his grip on her waist and framed her face, kissing her *grazioso*— gracefully. Just the melody. Like carefully picking out the notes one at time…discovering the song, writing it in the moment.

She deserved a sonata.

He couldn't break away. Couldn't stop tasting the sweetness, the goodness. He couldn't breathe. Didn't want to.

Suddenly, she pulled away before the symphony had been completed and touched her swollen lips. Eyes wide, she shook her head. "I—that—we can't."

They both knew this was a dead end from the start. He'd lost control.

His heart hammered, from a kiss so amazing he'd never forget it, and from fear of never gaining that control back where Cosette was concerned. "I'm sorry. I…" What? What could he possibly tell her?

She smoothed her hair and cleared her throat. "Let's be grown-ups. We're clearly attracted to one another and we've been side by side for the past couple weeks. More than ever. Emotions are running high."

That was an understatement. He studied her. Lipstick mostly gone, but some remained…how could that be? He shook the thought away. Before he could speak, she went on.

"And even if I did want to be romantically involved, I can't be with *you*."

The words from earlier were like a pop to the face with a wet, twisted hand towel.

He swallowed, couldn't catch his breath. "Right." He masked the hurt. "I'm controlling, obsessive, intrusive. And you work for me."

A pinched look crossed her face, but then her shoulders slumped. "Yes," she whispered. "But that's not all, Wilder. Tell me why you hold on to Allie through Renny. Why you still keep those dice in your glove box."

"I did."

"You talk in anecdotes. I want full-on transparency."

He wasn't going to give her that. After tonight, he couldn't if he wanted to. He was supposed to make her feel safe and he'd almost been killed. When her adrenaline crashed, she might think he was weak, and if he gave her full-on transparency, she'd definitely think that. He would not lose her respect and admiration. "I have nothing to share." The words tasted like bitter defeat.

Cosette sighed with resignation. "Don't kiss me again." She slipped from the office. The sun had begun to rise, but inside, Wilder felt like night would never end.

A knock broke the silence. Beckett Marsh entered. "Wheezer called us. We're all here. I saw the rubble. You okay?"

Wilder turned and Beckett's eyes widened.

"What?"

Beckett slowly shook his head. "Nothin'."

"I'm fine. It looks worse than it is." He couldn't bring himself to admit the guy in the stable got the jump on him. "I've been in here racking my brain. Let's toss out the who and talk about the why. Why would someone want to burn down an old stable? What would that accomplish? Unless it was meant to bring Cosette outside to be abducted. But she did come outside and no one took her. I was out of commission. Beau is dead. Kariss committed suicide—but I think that may have been homicide.

She either knew who took her car or she agreed to run down Cosette. Either way, someone cut a loose thread."

Beckett pursed his lips and rapidly blinked.

"What is wrong with you?"

Clearing his throat, Beckett rubbed his eyebrow. "Nothing. It's just hard to take you seriously when you're wearing lipstick." He tamped down a chuckle. "Red's a good color for you."

Wilder rubbed his lips, peeked at his hand. Cherry red. He opened his mouth. He had nothing. The kiss had been exposed. "It's not what you think." He strode to the door.

"I hope it is! If you're wearing lipstick for any other reason, we have a serious problem."

Wilder ignored Beckett's laughter coming from his office and stalked to the foyer, passing Shepherd Lightman.

"Hey, you all right—*dude*, did you know you have on lipstick?"

Wilder growled and blasted out the front door, swiping his lips. He wanted another look around the stable and the woods.

Get focused, Wilder. Do your job. Erase the memory of the kiss.

That wasn't going to happen. That kiss was absolutely without a doubt unforgettable.

He prowled the perimeter. Nothing out of the ordinary. Anyone could have hiked into the woods. And the more he thought about it, the less he believed it was Frank. Someone had to have set him up. Which meant CCM was being watched. Maybe he needed to add more cameras in the woods. Yes, that's exactly what he'd do. Beef up the surrounding area. Anyone slinking about out here would be caught.

Back inside, Shep handed him a cup of steaming coffee. "I guess you'll want extra cameras in the woods."

"You read my mind."

"It's what I'd do." He shrugged.

Evan entered, his heavy footfalls clanking along the wooden floor. "I can get on that today."

"I'll light a fire under the PD's backside to see if prints were found in Cosette's apartment." Shep sipped his coffee. "You think this Levitts guy could have figured out Cosette was going to expand the stable?"

Build it from ground-up now. "I don't know how."

"Money talks," Shep said. "Maybe he paid Frank for eavesdropping."

Beckett turned the corner and came into the foyer. "What's going on?"

"Conference room." Wilder motioned and they entered the dining room-turned-meeting area and sat at the long table. "Shep thinks Frank might be on Levitts's payroll for information."

"He tells Levitts about the new business about to happen, and Levitts either hires him or steals his hat and puts on painter's clothes to burn down the place. But why?" Shep asked.

Wilder spotted Cosette lurking. She'd cleaned up. He needed to.

"Starting a new business would stir him up," she said. "Burning the stable is his way of denying me any kind of life outside of him. I don't belong here. I belong to him. With him." Weariness and defeat colored her eyes.

"I'm going to find him. I can do it legally or I can change tactics and find him my way." Wilder waited for her permission to finally go at it like he wanted. Swiftly. Wheezer could hack finances. See where he'd been spending money. Trace him.

"As much as I want him found and this to be over, I

can't afford to go outside the legal bounds," she replied. "Not if I want to see him put in prison."

No one was going to get out of this unscathed. If Levitts thought Wilder was going to take a shovel to the head and not do anything about it, he was sorely mistaken. "Okay. We'll stay within legal bounds." But he ground his teeth and balled his fist.

They had to wait on prints from Kariss's car. If she hadn't been driving, whoever was might have left some. They were waiting on prints from Cosette's apartment, as well. Waiting on Levitts's next move. Waiting was killing Wilder.

Checking his watch, he found it was almost 6:00 a.m. "I'm gonna shower. Painting crew will be here in thirty minutes. If Frank shows up, I want you to descend on him like buzzards. If not, I'm not stopping until I find him. Today."

Cosette caught him at the door to his apartment. "I'm sorry. For calling you stupid in your office." A sheepish smile crept across her face. "For being…mouthy."

The word drew his attention to her full lips and he ached for another round of kissing. He couldn't stay mad. Lightly, he clipped her chin instead of opting for intruding on her mouth. "And I should have said thank you."

She grinned. "Yes, you should have."

He chuckled. "Truce?"

"Truce."

"Wanna seal it with a kiss?" he teased.

Cosette gave him a wooden look. "I'm off my emotional high."

He wasn't. "I'm a private person, Cosette. I can't help it. And I'm sorry things got out of hand—with the kiss. I know kissing means commitment."

"It does. And the only person I'm committed to is myself. Even if I could get past the other things, Wilder, I'd need you to be less private. Could you be?"

He wanted to be. "No."

She touched his forearm. "I understand." Translation: then that's that.

She left him at the door. Time to shower the dirt, grime and frustration away. Thirty minutes later, the painting crew pulled up, with Frank in the passenger side of the truck.

Time to put his feet to the fire.

Wilder bounded off the porch toward where they parked. "Frank, let's have us a chat." He gripped the man's shoulder and directed him into the house to his office, where Beckett, Shepherd and Cosette waited.

"What's goin' on, boss?" Frank asked and slid his gaze to each team member present.

"You like movies?" Wilder asked. "I've got a great one." He cued up the footage and hit Play.

Cosette kept her eye on Frank. Watching his reaction, body language, facial features.

At first, he frowned as if confused, but as the video continued he recognized what was happening. He jumped up. "That is not me, Mr. Flynn!"

"Is that your hat?"

"Yeah, but that went missing yesterday at lunch."

Wilder cut his eyes at Beckett. "Well, that's mighty convenient."

"It's t-true," Frank stammered. "I eat at the Blue Café most days. I had to go to the john and left my hat on the table. I came back and it was gone. I even asked the waitress about it. You can check that."

Frank didn't seem smart enough to ask the server about it to throw them off. Wilder looked to Cosette. He read her eyes. It appeared Frank was telling the truth.

"What was that waitress's name?"

"Kelly."

"If you'll excuse me," Beckett said and held his phone up behind Frank's head. He was going to call and check it out.

"Mr. Flynn, I'm not a rocket scientist. But I'm not dumb enough to bite the hand that feeds me. I have nothing to gain from burning down your stable."

"Have you been approached by a man lately concerning Miss LaCroix?" Wilder asked.

Frank shifted his attention to Cosette, confusion crinkling the lines around his eyes. "No," he said warily.

"Then someone followed you. Stole your hat. Wore painter's gear and a mask and framed you." Wilder pointed to the video screen. "Wouldn't you agree?"

"But why?"

That was the million-dollar question.

Beckett returned and nodded. Frank's story had checked out. If it wasn't a planted story.

"Mr. Flynn, on my honor, I didn't do this."

Wilder believed him, but until he knew for sure, the man couldn't stay on his property. "Frank, I want to take you at your word. We're going to do some more investigating and when we fully clear you, the paint will be here. Until then, I'm afraid I'll have to suspend the work."

"I understand. I'll tell my crew and we'll be on our way. Don't hold nothing against ya. I'd do whatever was necessary to protect my lady, too." He slipped from the room, escorted by Shepherd.

Cosette wasn't his lady, but no one in the room said a word. "Cosette?"

"Direct eye contact. Genuine surprise. That's hard to fake, especially when you have a group of former SEALS and a marine sniper in the room. He was nervous and fidgety, but I felt it was more due to fear of you and the team and what you might do to him than getting caught. He didn't respond like a guilty man."

Wilder trusted her professional judgment. "Beck, see if there's cameras at the Blue Café." He texted Shepherd to tail Frank for the next twelve hours, then switch off with Jody for the next twelve. He wanted to know where that man was going at all times of the day and night.

Picking up the phone, he called his contact at the Atlanta PD and inquired about the prints. A few minutes later he hung up. "Nothing popped."

"So now what?"

Wheezer poked his head in the office. "A detective Monty Chase is here to see you and Cosette."

Great. The same detective who had accompanied Detective Bodine from New Orleans. "Send him in."

Cosette licked her lips and perched on the chair next to Wilder's desk.

Detective Chase entered. "Mr. Flynn. Miss LaCroix."

"What can we do for you, Detective?" Wilder asked.

"I'm here about Kariss Elroy." He focused on Cosette. "She was a patient of yours?"

"Yes. For over a year."

"Medical examiner came back with the autopsy. We're ruling it homicide."

Cosette closed her eyes.

Wilder wanted to reach over and grasp her hand. Instead, he remained stoic. "Did she die from the carbon monoxide?"

"Yes."

"Then how do you know it was homicide?" Wilder asked.

"Miss LaCroix, did you prescribe her any meds? Xanax, to be specific? She had a lot of it in her system."

"I did not. And if she got her hands on it otherwise,

who's to say she didn't overdose herself, then go sit in the vehicle?"

"No trace of a Xanax bottle anywhere."

"She could have gotten them in a baggie from a dealer," Cosette offered.

"Maybe," the detective said. "But that wouldn't explain the bruising around her neck and wrists. Someone did that. Maybe that dealer using baggies."

"No need for that tone," Wilder said and stood. "We're trying to make sense of this as much as you are."

"I'm going to need alibis…again. A former boyfriend. Now a patient. Can you connect these two people together in any way, Miss LaCroix?"

"I have a theory." She looked to Wilder for support. He gave her the go-ahead with a nod.

She told him everything that had happened since their first encounter and how she believed that Jeffrey had escalated. Wilder filled him in on the stable burning and someone knocking him out. "He's on a medical leave of absence. We haven't been able to locate him. He's away from his apartment, and like I said before, we're trying to be discreet."

The detective pocketed the slip of information. "I looked into him myself, but he's squeaky clean."

"I assure you, he's not," Cossette said.

Wilder walked him to the door. He hadn't believed them last time and he wasn't picking up what they were putting down now.

Time would tell.

EIGHT

Cosette stood at the stable ash pile and relived what happened three nights ago. Wilder's body lying lifeless. Her dream destroyed. Until Jeffrey was apprehended, she'd never be free. Never be able to stop looking back. Her life was in a prison. Like her father's. His attorney had called two more times since the stable had burned and she'd ignored them, but hadn't blocked him. Some teensy part of her was curious, wanted to obey God's instructions to forgive. His conviction was always hovering no matter how hard she tried to escape it. It came loud and soft. Demanding but coaxing.

Jody's words about forgiveness continued to grip her heart. Forgiving was for Cosette and her freedom. Freedom to move on. To let go of the past. But mixed in with that pain and those reminders of nights she'd cowered in a room, afraid Dad was going to storm in and lash out at her, she also had some fond memories. The frightening memories always outweighed them. But they were there.

Crawfish boils, swimming in lakes, hot summer nights. Humidity never bothered her. Laughing with friends. Boating on the bayou. Cokes in glass bottles at Grandma's. Fishing on pontoon boats. Sundays fanning herself with the bulletins and listening to the preacher talk of faith, hope and love. She'd given her life to Jesus as a child. Somewhere between faith and fear, she'd lost her way. Her need for security and love led her down a crooked path. A path that looked well-lit, only to be utter darkness. So many mistakes had been made. And then Dad went into a drunken rage and Mama took a tumble down the wooden stairs at his hands.

Manslaughter.

The crunching of grass brought her spinning around. Wilder approached. The man could wear jeans like no other. She swallowed and cleared her throat. He carried a rolled-up paper in his hand. "Whatcha doin' out here? It's almost nightfall."

As if he didn't know exactly where she was. He'd probably been watching her on a monitor from his office.

"Just looking at what was," she sighed. "Until Jeffrey is found and put away, he'll keep coming. Keep burning down all my hopes. All my dreams. He'll keep my future in flames until nothing is left."

Wilder stood next to her and looked at the piles of ash. "That seems hopeless. Since when did you stop looking on the bright side?"

"Since it stopped being bright." She pointed to his paper. "What's that?"

"The bright side." His grin sent her tummy into flight. "Cosette, if you think I'm going to let a stalker rob you of your joy and future, you really don't know me at all."

"We keep saying that to one another. I think it's because deep down, we know it's true. You might know my favorite cake flavor and what I like to drink at the coffee shop, and you know my personal past because of a background check. But you don't *know* me. And I sure don't know you."

He kicked at the dirt. "I know you love people more than yourself. You'll go on fumes if that's what it takes to make someone well. You never buy yourself anything, just because. You save every penny you can because you want this equine therapy. Again, confirming you love others more than yourself. I know that your father broke your heart and your family, but you climbed out of that pit—not without emotional scars—and made something of yourself. You refused to be a statistic. You're a perfectionist, which as a boss I happen to love."

She couldn't help her smile.

"You sleep with your face buried in a pillow. I have lipstick stains on mine to prove it. I also know that as much as you hated your childhood, you've hung on to it or that jewelry box wouldn't have stayed on your dresser all these years. You have photos of you and your mom in your apartment—those are memories."

Wilder was astute. He did know her. What could she say about him? "All I know is you hide things, Wilder."

"That's not true and you know it. But you're right. Some things *can't* be told. Some things are classified."

"Not all things."

Wilder shoved a hand in his pocket. "I hang on to the dice to hang on to Alan. To remind me of who I am supposed to be—a protector. If I hadn't gone in a ditch, Alan would be alive."

A step in the right direction. "You feel that way, but it's not true. You can't control life, Wilder. You aren't God." If he hung on to the dice for that reason... "Is that why you hang on to Renny? To hang on to Allie?"

"I suppose." His jaw ticked and he gestured with the rolled-up paper. "The bright side."

"Why can't you just tell me what happened? Do you think I'll judge you?"

Wilder slapped the paper on his palm a few times, then held it out. "I see no point in drudging up the past. I'd rather focus on the future."

Frustration wound tight around her chest. "Fine. Let's

focus on the future." A future that was a moot point with Jeffrey out there. "What is this?"

"Blueprints. For a new stable, office and reflection pond. I read they're relaxing and beneficial." He pointed beyond the pile of ashes. "I thought they could dig it out that way. Build a bridge over it. Maybe you could use it as a metaphor. Building a bridge from the past to the future."

Cosette was wrong. She did know Wilder. Not his past, but his heart. Tough as nails. Tender as spring grass. Loyal. Protective. Fierce. Tenacious.

Blinking back hot tears and swallowing the lump in her throat, she clasped his big, warm hand. "You're a good man, Wilder Flynn." Even with his flaws. His added ideas only proved how important this equine therapy was and how much she needed this job. A relationship with Wilder could jeopardize that. "I appreciate that you took time to research it. It's a great idea."

"Good." He patted the blueprints in his hand again. "My family is cooking out tonight. Come with me and we'll look at the blueprints and set up a time to go check out those quarter horses again. Have you talked to the Abrams woman?"

"I have, actually." She fell into step with him as they strode to the house. "I told her things were on hold for now, but her offer for me to fly out and talk is still open. She's really a sweet lady."

"I want to ask you something."

"Okay."

"Can we please skirt the law and find this guy? Just to know his location. We don't have to approach him. Just…locate him."

Cosette wanted to scream yes, but Wilder wouldn't stop there. "And if he's in a hotel ten minutes from here, you'll leave him there? Unapproached?"

"Unapproached."

Cosette grinned. "But not alone."

"I'll put eyes on him. Yes. Then we catch him dead to rights. I don't like hearing you talk about your life being in limbo, with no future. You've had enough. If we can connect him through financials to New Orleans and here, we might be able to connect him to the murder of Beau and Kariss. Let's be honest, the police are looking at you and me for that right now."

As they approached the house, a car pulled into the circle drive and Cosette groaned. "I know that car."

Wilder heaved a sigh. The door opened and Detective Chase got out. "Were your ears burning, Detective? We were just talking about you."

Detective Chase sucked his top teeth. "Burning is why I'm here."

"You talking about the stable?" Wilder asked.

"Nope." He messed with the collar of his button-up shirt. "Can we talk in the air-conditioning?"

Wilder nodded and led him inside to the conference room.

Cosette tried not to fidget. She'd appear guilty. "Would you like a glass of lemonade or water?"

"No, thank you. Can you tell me the last time you spoke to or saw Malcolm Hayes? I'm aware he's also a patient of yours."

Cosette's stomach roiled. "Has he been harmed?"

Detective Chase opened his notepad. "He burned down his apartment, and most of the building in the process, last night."

She'd encouraged him on several occasions to rent a house. She'd feared if he set his apartment ablaze, lives would be taken. "How many were hurt?"

"Most of the tenants got out alive. Minor injuries,

some smoke inhalation. Unfortunately, Malcolm wasn't one of them. He was killed in the fire."

Cosette covered her mouth, afraid she might be sick. "He suffered from pyromania." She was no longer bound to confidentiality.

Wilder crossed his ankle over his knee. "Why the drive out here to tell us one of her patients suffering from pyromania died in a fire he started?"

"ME is doing the autopsy. Can't rule out accident just yet." He eyed Cosette. "You think that boy burned down your stable?"

Wilder looked at Cosette. She tried for a brave face, but it was faltering. Two of her patients were dead. What was happening?

"I'm not saying he couldn't have. But he wouldn't have stolen the painter's hat and dressed like a painter. His desire to set something ablaze isn't calculated. It's not intended to murder or hurt people. It's a disease."

"You think this Jeffrey Levitts did it? Like the other crimes?"

"I do," Cosette said. "I have no patients obsessed with me. No one in my life who might be suspect. We've already had this discussion. We also suspected Beau at first. But now we believe Jeffrey murdered Beau. Maybe Kariss, too."

"You must be fearful, Miss LaCroix. Ready to make this go away."

"More than you—"

"Stop!" Wilder said, his hand raised. He stood. "Don't say another word, Cosette." He narrowed his eyes and locked them on Detective Chase. "What aren't you telling us?"

"Malcolm Hayes wasn't the only one dead in the fire.

We've identified the other body in his apartment as Jeffrey Levitts."

Cosette slumped in the chair, her mouth hanging open. Jeffrey was dead? How? How did they all connect? "Are you...are you sure?"

"Partial remains of a wallet says so and we're running dental records. Should have something soon." He ran his teeth along his bottom lip. "I'm going to ask if you'll ride with me to the station for further questioning."

"Ask them here." Wilder laid a hand on Cosette's shoulder.

"I can have her come as a formality or I can arrest her. I have grounds." Detective Chase stood. "Beau Chauvert threatened you. Kariss Elroy tried to run you down and Malcolm... Malcolm may well have burned down your stable or done something I don't know about yet. They're all dead now. Miss LaCroix, you have motive."

"Well, so did Jeffrey Levitts, if he was using them as pawns."

"And yet Jeffrey Levitts is now dead, too. So no one really knows what his part in all of this was. No one is left but you, Miss LaCroix."

Cosette stood, but her knees buckled until Wilder stepped to her side and kept her upright. "I didn't do this. I would never take a life." Was she being framed by someone else?

Wilder clutched her shoulders. "Go with Detective Chase. Say nothing. I'll call Aurora and we'll meet you at the precinct. This is going to be okay. I promise."

Detective Chase had come to arrest her all along. They had no hard evidence. Only circumstantial, but it was enough to hold her. Enough to try and scare her, and it was working.

How had Jeffrey managed to get into Malcolm's apartment? Did he talk Malcolm into burning down the stable? If he knew her client was a pyro, it wouldn't have been difficult. He'd have used mind games on him. But how had he ended up dead?

Wilder framed Cosette's face. "Be brave, darlin'. I'm right behind you." He kissed her forehead.

Cosette struggled to breathe. She'd never been arrested. Never been held for any reason. This looked bad. If it got out, she could lose her job. Her reputation. Was that Jeffrey's plan all along? Then he could swoop in and offer to whisk her away, back to Washington, where a prestigious job would be waiting for her. Jeffrey would be her hero. She'd owe him. Love him.

"I'm scared," she whispered in Wilder's ear as he hugged her.

He stroked her hair. "I know. It's okay, though. They have nothing. I'll call my contact at the department and handle it." He squeezed her tightly. "Hour tops and you'll be out of there. Aurora will see to that. She'll be fit to be tied."

Thankfully, Aurora had her license to practice in Georgia. Cosette had never dreamed she'd be needing her as a defense attorney. "I'll be brave because I trust you to come get me and keep me safe."

"I won't let you down."

"Miss LaCroix…"

Cosette followed Detective Chase to his vehicle.

"You can sit in front," he said. "Courtesy."

"Thanks." Her flat tone said it all. "I don't know why you're doing this. I didn't do anything. You're looking at the wrong person."

"Says the only one alive."

It did look bad. As bad as it could. Did something go wrong with Jeffrey's plan? Could there be someone else behind this? Someone else working with Jeffrey, or alone?

Detective Chase barreled down the long drive from CCM and turned left onto the back road that led to the interstate. Cosette reeled. Jeffrey was dead. But this didn't feel over.

A popping sound dragged her from her thoughts.

"Hold on! Tire blew." Detective Chase gripped the wheel. Glass shattered. Blood sprayed across the windshield and Cosette shrieked and instinctively ducked.

Detective Chase stared blankly, his head lolling to the side.

The tire hadn't blown. It had been shot out. Just like the back window, where a bullet had zinged through and hit Detective Chase.

Cosette grabbed the wheel, her head pounding. She was headed straight for the ditch. Yanking the wheel hard to the right, she tried to swerve away from a tree, but wasn't on time.

The car smacked into the trunk with brute force and the airbag blew.

And Cosette saw only darkness.

Wilder rushed into the control room. "Wheezer, I need you to work fast and hard. I want all financials on Jeffrey Levitts." He was dead, so invading his private accounts was on the table now. "If he's used a check, debit or credit card, I want to know where. I want to know when and I want to know what he purchased, even if it was a pack of nabs."

Wheezer wheeled his chair around and went to work clacking keys, no questions asked.

Shepherd stormed into the room with Evan on his heels. "What do you need from us?"

"I don't know yet." Wilder pawed his face. "Help me connect the dots. What are we missing?"

Shepherd pulled out the whiteboard and grabbed a dry-erase marker. He wrote Cosette's name in the middle, then drew lines to each person she was connected to. "Wheezer, see if you can find a connection between any or all of these people. Evan, you take over financials."

Evan grabbed a chair and took the laptop Wheezer had been using to hack Levitts's finances. "Jody will be here in twenty minutes."

Wheezer nodded, typed furiously and swung around to another computer. "Social media is a good place to start. We'll see if any of them are friends."

Kariss and Malcolm could have met outside the clinic and become friends or more. Jeffrey could have seen them as two birds, one stone. But how did he end up dead? That didn't make sense. What weren't they seeing? Had he and Malcolm fought over the fire in the stable and it had ended badly? Had Malcolm approached him about Kariss and it escalated? Wilder growled and fisted his hand.

"Where is Aurora? I called her twenty minutes ago!" Cosette would be going out of her mind. He had to get her out of this. Rescue her.

"She's at a doctor's appointment. Beckett took her. Baby picture today. Chill. It's not like Cosette's not safe with the police." Shepherd tapped the marker in his palm and stared at the board.

"Nothing on any social media sites," Wheezer muttered. "Not even a friend of a friend. I'm going to see if any of them have friends in New Orleans or Washington. Maybe I can track a connection that way."

Wilder paced the floor like a caged animal. He

grabbed his cell phone and called Teddy. She answered on the first ring.

"Teddy, I need a favor."

"Of course you do." She crunched into something.

"That robe and the house shoes at Levitts's place. Cosette says they're not hers. Can you find out if he's dated anyone in the time that Cosette has been gone? That's odd. What woman would leave her night stuff there and allow him to have photos of him and Cosette all over the place?"

"None. He hasn't been here since his leave of absence. I'll stop off at his place of work."

Wheezer popped up. "Levitts's social media says he's in a complicated relationship."

"Find out with who."

Nodding, Wheezer went to work hacking. A few minutes later, he pumped his fist in the air. "I'm in." He scrolled the social media site. "He has a picture with a woman he dated about a year back. I see nothing of Cosette."

"Find the woman."

"Found. Lisa Jackson. Her site is set to private. No personal information."

"Find a number. Yesterday! Maybe she knows something."

Wilder's phone rang. Jody. "Where are you?"

"Wilder." Her voice shook and she cleared her throat. "I'm about two miles from the house. Long story short, I'm standing in neck-high weeds and looking at a dead Detective Chase. Cosette's been taken."

NINE

Wilder's heart beat at lightning speed as he bolted from the office to the SUV. Beckett had finally arrived with Aurora and was hot on his heels. "Wilder, calm down."

"Calm down?" How was he supposed to remain calm? The woman he loved had been abducted.

There it was. The words to his feelings. He loved her. And he'd failed her.

She looked to him to keep her safe. To come for her. He had zero control right now. No clue who had her. Where they might be. What might be happening to her.

He should have immediately followed and not waited on Aurora. He'd forgotten she'd had a doctor's appointment. Who had taken Cosette? Couldn't be Jeffrey Levitts. He was dead. No doubt the dental records would confirm it.

Beckett jumped in the passenger seat and Wilder peeled out the drive and to the site where Jody waited. He wanted to beat the police to the scene. Jody's vehicle was up ahead. Wilder slammed on the brakes and parked, then jumped from the SUV and raced to the detective's car.

Cosette's purse was on the floorboard. He took it and checked her phone. "It's password protected." What would she use? Her birthday. *Boom.* He was in. He scrolled through her texts. Nothing out of the ordinary. No further weird calls. Just several phone calls from her dad's lawyer.

"Someone shot out the tire, then fired two more rounds into the back windshield. Not a bad shot. He clearly wasn't aiming for Cosette," Jody said.

Of course he wasn't. He wanted her all to himself. The lipstick heart. The notes about missing her and loving her. Wilder's stomach clenched. If this man laid one hand on her, so help him... Spots formed in front of him. He was literally seeing red.

"Wilder. I know that look. Relax." Beckett held eye contact with him. "We're going to find her. Levelheadedness will get us there. You showed me that."

Fear coupled with fury broke out in sweat droplets on his forehead and spine. Sirens wailed in the distance.

It had been about an hour since Cosette left the house. Whoever had her was racing with time on their side. They'd vanished.

Wilder's lungs squeezed. He couldn't think straight. Images of what might be happening to Cosette consumed him until he shook uncontrollably. She was counting on him. They all were counting on him.

He blinked and realized he was in the passenger side of the SUV. Beckett was pulling into the circle drive at CCM. Had time slipped? He didn't even remember talking with the police on the scene, but he must have. He was losing it. Fighting to muster control and strength, he squeezed his eyes shut and prayed.

God, where is she?

"Wilder."

Wilder ignored Beckett and slunk up the porch steps and into the house, where he fell to his knees. All the pain, every weight he'd been carrying, every secret he'd pushed aside came crashing down on his heart at once, sucking oxygen from him and leaving him cold, weak.

Alone.

His mind kept screaming at him to get up. He was a soldier, a navy SEAL, a leader. A fighter. He was responsible for this team. His family. His clients. Cosette.

But no matter how much he told himself to stand at attention and pull it together, he couldn't muster the strength to stand—to speak.

Cosette was gone.

Lost.

And it was all his fault. Tears burned the back of his eyes. A fresh cold sweat broke out.

"He can't breathe," someone said. The voices were muffled, as if he was miles away and locked in a cavernous prison. "Get a paper bag."

"Dude, you're scaring me."

"Get him some water."

"Wilder!"

"Should I slap his face?"

"Not if you want to live."

With his hands on the floor to hold himself up, he gasped for air. His team was seeing this and yet he couldn't stop it. What if Cosette died? He hadn't even had the chance to tell her he loved her. So much.

But she didn't love him. And she'd surely add weak to her list of flaws for him.

He *was* weak. He couldn't even get off the floor.

His eyes burned and filled with moisture.

"Wilder, breathe into this. Deep." Aurora. She was placing a lunch sack over his mouth. Someone rubbed his back. "Keep breathing. We'll find her. It's okay."

Beckett prayed over him, then spoke. "Wilder, I know how you feel. You think it's your fault. But it's not."

He shoved the paper bag away and stood. "Yes, it is. It's all my fault. Allie. Meghan."

Beckett's eyes clouded. "How is Meghan your fault?"

He swallowed the lump in this throat and looked around at his team members. Members he was supposed to be protecting and leading. "I was there," he whispered. "She was alive, Beck. Barely and for only seconds, but she was."

Beckett's face turned pale. "What?"

Wilder told him about that night as he wiped away tears of weakness, regret and grief over his sister. "I couldn't save her."

Beckett stood there stunned. Aurora put her arm around him to bring comfort. The one woman who could comfort Wilder was gone.

"Wilder..." Beckett finally spoke. "I need to process this, but what I do know right now is that you can't blame yourself for not saving her any more than I can. God controls everything. I don't have answers to why, but I don't have to have them to know He's got everything in the palm of His hand."

Wilder could barely hold his head up. He'd revealed how pitifully weak he was. "I'm sorry. I've failed you." With that he jumped up, hurried to his office and stared at the whiteboard. Cosette could be anywhere.

His entire team followed him, Jody at the helm. "Wilder, you're our leader," she said. "Our boss, not our God. We don't expect you to always know the answers. To always get it right. We're a family. We stand united. We fall united. Do you understand that?"

He scanned each face and found no judgment.

Had he been playing God? When he couldn't save Allie or Meghan, he hadn't questioned God or even been mad at Him. Wilder had questioned and been mad at himself for not controlling the situation and rescuing them. Maybe he'd expected more of himself than he did God. He shook his head, stunned at what his heart conveyed.

"You're not weak, Wilder, you're human," Evan said softly.

But he didn't see himself that way. Never had. Not since he was three years old and his father laid the responsibility on him for protecting Meghan and then Caley.

"Let's rally and find our headshrinker," Shepherd stated.

Wilder couldn't find words to say and right now it didn't matter. He had to pull it together. "I should have covered every base. But I trusted Cosette—I do trust her. She said it was Jeffrey and I believe her, but he's dead and someone took her. Who? Why?" He and Cosette had both made mistakes and it was costing him time and possibly her life.

"It could have been Levitts stalking her, but maybe he needed help from someone. Someone he could manipulate and deceive. Maybe this person found out what he was really up to and killed him." Jody perched on the edge of Wilder's desk. "The part that remains unclear is where Malcolm Hayes and Kariss Elroy fit in."

"I think our initial speculation, that Levitts used Kariss as a pawn with the muffins and the car, is our best option. And he probably did get Malcolm to burn down the stable. Killing them to cover his tracks makes sense. But somehow he was betrayed by another person and was killed, too." Wilder raked his hands through his hair. Hair he wanted Cosette to touch again. Only she'd made her feelings clear. But that kiss…that was more than heightened emotion. Or was he just feeling what he wished was there?

Jody splayed her hands in front of her. "Whoever it is would have to be equally or more cunning than Levitts. Someone who could fake being pliable to Jeffrey's whims and plans."

"It'd have to be someone who would know which patients could be used. Because he had access to them and to Cosette," Beckett offered.

Wilder gripped the desk. "A colleague. Wheezer, check and see if Levitts had any kind of connection to any of the other doctors or staff at the clinic. Make sure to do a thorough check on Dr. McMillian and Roger Renfrow. Dig deeper than our initial search." When Cosette had come clean, Wilder had had Wheezer do a background check on the staff and doctors at the clinic. Nothing had raised a red flag. Now it was time to look under rugs and in the back of closets. They should have done this earlier, anyway.

Wheezer grunted. "This will take more than a minute, Wilder."

A minute more than they had.

"Wilder," Jody said. "If Cosette had to ask for time off from you, then she'd have to ask her boss at the clinic, too. She works some Fridays and occasionally Saturdays when she's not here."

Dr. Irwin McMillian.

Wilder wasn't waiting on data.

"Wheezer, get his home number and address. Call it."

Wheezer went to work, then made the call. No answer. "I'll try the office. What do you want me to do if he answers?"

"Hang up."

A few seconds later, Wheezer hung up and nodded. "He's there." He then called Renfrow's home. No answer. He might be at the clinic, as well.

Cosette might be, too.

"Evan, Wheezer, stay here and keep looking at finan-

cials and possible online connections. If you can find a
way to get files from the clinic's mainframe, do it. Do
whatever you have to. I don't care about legalities." Only
finding Cosette. "Beck and I will go to the clinic. Jody,
Shepherd, try Roger's home. He may not be answering
for a reason."

Twenty minutes later, Wilder and Beckett busted into
the clinic. "Offices are down this hall." They strode to
Dr. McMillian's office. Wilder didn't bother knocking.

The doctor startled. He was a tall man with a receding
hairline and friendly face. If he had Cosette, he'd hidden
her somewhere.

"Can I help you?"

"Do you know where Cosette is?" Wilder asked and
reached for his sidearm. "I'd think real hard before you
lie to me."

McMillian raised his hands and slowly stood. "Let's
all just calm down," he said, in a tone he would obviously
use on a panicked patient. Well, Wilder was panicked,
and at this point he'd do whatever necessary to get Cosette back. Every minute they were losing time. "Cosette
canceled her client appointments due to a personal issue.
Which you know. I recognize you, Mr. Flynn."

"Has she told you the personal issue?" Beckett asked.

McMillian remained stoic. "No, but I'm not her personal therapist or a confidant."

"Short story. Someone is stalking her and she was abducted over an hour ago."

The doc's eyes widened. "What can I do to help?"

Wilder wasn't sold on his innocence just yet. "You're
the only one who would know about her visiting New Orleans each Mother's Day. Whoever took her has to know
this, too." Now that he thought about it, the dog being
here and the letter were mighty convenient. "Who was

working on the eighth?" Someone had to have access to her office in order to get the letter inside.

McMillian fired up his computer. "Everyone was."

Roger. He had the puppy. He was the first to arrive. He knew Cosette took off work every Mother's Day weekend. Right now, Wilder couldn't connect him to Levitts or his death, but Wilder hadn't liked him from the start and it wasn't just because he wore a bow tie. "Renfrow. He here today at all?"

"Roger? No, actually. He called in sick for the rest of the week."

That was way too convenient for Wilder's liking. He called Jody. "ETA on Renfrow's house now."

"We're stuck on the interstate. Car accident."

Wilder growled and hung up, then called Wheezer. "Alternate route to Renfrow's from the clinic. Now."

Wheezer clacked keys and rattled off directions. Wilder hung up and addressed Dr. McMillian. "If I find out you're lying to me about anything, I will come back. What I do will be slow. Painful. And you will regret it for eternity."

"You don't have to use violent threats, Mr. Flynn. I'm not involved, and I want to help. But I don't believe Roger has abducted Cosette. You should consider diplomacy with him."

Wilder didn't bother with a reply and stormed out with Beck behind him.

"You were kidding about torturing him to death, right?" Beck asked.

"What do you think?"

"I think I hope he's not lying." Beckett put his hand on Wilder's shoulder. "I think I should drive and you should empty your magazine and chamber."

Wilder huffed and climbed in the passenger seat.

Roger Renfrow. He had access to Kariss Elroy and Malcolm Hayes. He knew their mental states. Cosette and he were friends, so he would know personal things about her. Like nut allergies. Her past, if not in detail, at least enough. But why say he missed her? That part didn't compute. Unless he was crazy, and crazy never computed. He made more sense than Jeffrey enlisting a patient to do his dirty work, but Wilder wasn't going to rule anything out just yet.

"What did you think about McMillian?" Beckett asked.

"I don't know." Wilder was frustrated, and everyone was suspect. He needed clarity. "Let's go in with the assumption that Renfrow has Cosette and this is a rescue mission. Night will cover us. Keep neighbors from getting nosy."

"Do you think he'd have her at his house? I mean, he killed a detective and surely he knows we'd eventually figure it out," Beckett said.

Wilder didn't have the answer to that, either. Didn't need to at the moment. "We'll proceed with caution. That's all we can do." He hoped wherever Cosette was, she had a level head and could use her expertise to keep herself safe and alive.

They entered an older neighborhood. The lawns were manicured and the streets quiet. Beckett parked a ways down from the house.

"Let's do a little recon. If we spook him, he might hurt her or worse," Beckett said. "And call Shep and Jody. Get an ETA."

Wilder called and they were ten minutes out. He drew his weapon. He never enjoyed using it, but in times like this—times of war—there was no choice.

They quietly slipped through the shadows into Roger's yard. Blinds were closed. No movement.

"House has a basement."

"Good place to hold a hostage," Wilder whispered. They crept to the other side of the property. Sounds of a TV came from a window. Bedroom, probably. "Let's bust up in there."

"And if he's innocent, he'll (1) have a heart attack and (2) sue us and have us arrested for home invasion." Beckett drilled him with a glare. "What happened to proceed with caution?"

"We did. I also said this was a rescue mission. What if it was Aurora?"

Beckett sighed. "Okay. Let's knock down a door."

Rustling sounded and a low whistle. It was Shep and Jody. They'd made it. Jogging up, Shep asked, "What's the plan?"

"Going through the front door," Beckett said.

Jody opened her mouth, but Shepherd spoke. "If he's guilty, he'll run. If he's innocent, you'll scare him. And he'll run. We'll be at the back. Waiting on Red Rover to send the headshrinker right over."

Wilder looked at Beckett as they stood on the porch. "If he's…done anything to her, I can't promise I won't kill him." His voice cracked as his throat clogged with emotion. "Do you understand?"

Beckett nodded. "You're my best friend. My brother. I won't let you slip away. I've got your six in every way. Now break this door down and get your woman."

My woman.

Cosette would hate that phrase with a passion. But Wilder wanted her to be his. Not a possession. A partner.

But he'd failed her. She'd trusted him. Trusted his

word. He'd told her it would be okay. To go with Detective Chase.

"Ready?"

Beckett secured his gun. "Go."

Wilder rammed his shoulder into the door with all his might; the wood splintered, cracked and burst open, revealing a tidy home, the smells of lemon and vapor rub. Was Jody in here already? She kept that stuff on her nose constantly to block out overwhelming scents due to her medical condition.

He raced through the living room toward the room with the TV.

Roger Renfrow bustled into the hallway shirtless, baseball bat in hand.

"That won't save you," Wilder growled. "Drop it."

Roger instantly complied. "What's going on?"

"Where is she?"

"Who?"

Wilder wound his hand around Roger's neck, smelled the vapor rub, pinned him against the wall. "Don't play with me."

"I don't know what is going on," the man said breathlessly.

Shepherd and Jody entered the hallway. "The house is clear, Wilder. She's not here. I don't even smell her," Jody said. If anyone could smell Cosette it would be Jody—a human bloodhound.

"Why weren't you at work today?" Wilder asked.

"I have bronchitis!"

"Nothing's here to make me think he's stalking Cosette," Shepherd said.

Renfrow's eyes bulged. "Stalking Cosette? Are you kidding me? I'm calling the police right now!"

Wilder laughed. "If you can get past me, feel free. I

have questions and you're going to answer them. Truthfully. Have you been sending Cosette gifts and messages?"

"No. But I had a feeling something strange was going on. Can you please release your grip before you crush my windpipe?"

Wilder released him, his hope sinking.

"At first, I thought you were abusive to her. She seemed to show signs," Roger stated.

"I would never lay a hand on her!" He had an urge to throttle the guy for even suggesting it.

"Yes, I can tell you're quite meek," he deadpanned. "I realized that wasn't the case and that you were protecting her from something. Someone. If someone has her, please let me help."

If this man was lying, he deserved an Oscar. And if he wasn't, who had Cosette?

Cosette's head felt like someone had stabbed it with a dagger. She opened her eyes and squinted through the sunlight pouring into the room. Dizzy and disoriented, she worked to put pieces together; it was fuzzy. The air-conditioning kicked on and she shivered and glanced upward. A vent blew cold air down on her. She blinked and tried to jump-start her muddled brain.

Detective Chase believed she'd killed Beau, Jeffrey and her patients. She'd been on her way to the police station when the officer's car had crashed.

No. He'd been shot and the car ran into a tree. She'd lost consciousness.

Her tongue was thick and seemed to be taking up her entire dry mouth. The room was too bright and blurry.

Someone had drugged her after she'd blacked out. The effects she was feeling had to be from a strong sedative.

Where was she?

Pale pink walls with white trim… A pink Victorian dollhouse sat on a small white table in the corner. Dolls had been arranged at a dining room table. The furniture was white, with antique scrolls, like someone had painted the wood finish, making it trendy for a little girl.

Grabbing her head, Cosette tried to sit up, but collapsed. She was in a four-poster twin bed that matched the snowy white furniture. On pink sheets with pale lavender hearts. A frilly comforter.

Why was she in a little girl's bedroom? Whose room?

She struggled to shake off the dizzy sensation. Nausea swept into her throat and her mouth watered. How long had she been out? After working herself into a sitting position, she swung her legs over the side of the bed and held still while her head swam. Her bare feet sunk into the plush carpet. Light blared through pink-and-white chevron curtains. She was upstairs. Somewhere.

A window meant escape.

Tottering to it, she glanced outside and shielded her eyes. She was in a subdivision. She couldn't see houses to the left or right, but there was a backyard with swings and a water play table. Beyond the wooden privacy fence, several houses on small lots dotted the area.

Her vision slowly cleared, but she was still woozy. Turning, she spied her ballerina jewelry box on the dresser. Her heart skipped a beat. Cosette caught a glimpse of her face in the mirror. Her lipstick was smeared like the Joker's in *Batman*. Her eye makeup had long worn off. And her wavy hair was knotted. She was a horror show all by herself.

She stumbled to the door and tried to open it.

Locked from the outside.

To the left was a small bathroom that matched the bedroom. All done in pink and lavender. She ran cool water and splashed her face. She needed all her faculties to be clear. She'd never get out of here in this fuzzy state. Using the lavender hand towel with a unicorn on it, she washed the lipstick away.

If she could get someone's attention behind the fence, she might be able to get out of here. Wherever *here* was.

She unlocked the window and raised it. Humidity smacked her freshly cooled face. Lifting the screen, Cosette stuck her head outside. It was quiet. Kids must be in school, adults at work. Below her lay two little-girl bikes.

"Help!" she croaked. It felt as if she hadn't used her voice in days. Could she have been knocked out that long?

She studied the room again. Something about it felt oddly familiar.

The jewelry box. It was hers, but it also belonged to... It was there on the tip of her tongue. She'd seen it. Here.

"Think, Cosette!" She racked her brain. A backpack hung from a hook by the door. She unzipped it and dug around inside. Pulling out a folder, she studied and found a name. "Daysia Carson." Didn't ring a bell. A library book was shoved in the bottom. She grabbed it and read the label. Her blood turned to ice. She wasn't even in Atlanta. She was in New Orleans.

Why would she be back here? She hadn't lived or worked here since her midtwenties. Had she been in this room before? Seemed like she had.

The jewelry box.

A bathroom. She remembered a bathroom.

Nothing more would come, but the fear that raised gooseflesh on her arms said it didn't matter. She'd find out soon enough.

She went back to the window and had opened her mouth to scream when the lock on the door clicked. Cosette hurriedly closed the window, then raced back to the bed and crawled inside. Her pulse pounded.

The door slowly opened.

Cosette gasped and her blood turned cold.

Wilder hadn't slept in the forty-eight hours Cosette had been missing. The gun that killed Detective Chase was a .45 caliber, but no match with ballistics. The police had no leads but were staying on it like white on rice since one of their own had been murdered. That gave him some small comfort, but his team wasn't any closer to figuring out who had her than they'd been the day they charged the clinic and busted down Roger Renfrow's front door. This was unacceptable. She couldn't have vanished from the face of the earth!

He bounced his knee as he sat next to Wheezer and Evan, both frantically typing on laptops in the control room of CCM.

They'd worked around the clock, digging up old clients and classmates, and going through all her past colleagues again, scrutinizing anyone who might have had a vendetta or attachment to Cosette. But nothing was tracking.

Any horrible thing could have happened to her by now. Wilder envisioned Cosette crying out for him and begging for her life, shaking with fear and hopelessness. Balling a fist, he stood and paced the floor. He was failing her every single second.

If she was even alive.

Terror struck with such force he nearly buckled to the floor. He couldn't think like that. She was alive, using her professional skills to stay that way. She had to be. "Please, tell me you have a lead. Anything?"

Their faces said it all. Nothing.

Jody entered with more coffee. They'd been living off

the stuff. No one had gone home; no one had slept. Every last one of them looked like death warmed over. Blood-shot eyes, disheveled hair… Wilder rubbed his chin. A full-on beard. Who had time to shave?

"Y'all. Roger Renfrow is here," Caley said. Wilder's baby sister had been here with Shepherd, taking care of him—of them all.

"Bring him in."

Roger, still recovering from bronchitis, entered the cramped control room. No bow tie. "I was hoping I could be of more assistance."

Two days ago, after they'd bombarded his home and nearly sent him into cardiac arrest, he'd helped with case files and tagged patients who might have become ob-sessed with Cosette. But none of those had panned out. As she'd said, no one fit the bill.

"We appreciate that," Wilder said. "But I don't know how."

Roger eyed the whiteboard and looked at all the dots they couldn't seem to connect. "What we know is some-one is obsessed with Cosette and has been strategically planning her abduction. However, this person went off script. How would anyone know the police were coming for her? I think they were watching, saw the police take her away, and it scared them. Foiled the perfect plan, and they went off the rails. Shot the detective and snatched her. They didn't realize or logically think out that the po-lice would suspect Cosette."

"That lines up with everything we've already estab-lished. Someone has been watching her. The idea of flip-ping the script makes sense. What we need is a name. Something that will lead us down the right path to find-ing her."

Roger agreed. "We keep running down clients who

might be romantically obsessed, but what if that's not the motive at all?"

Wilder stopped pacing. The man had his attention. "Go on."

"The letters, the gifts. Even the lipstick heart on the mirror. All seemed like romantic gestures, but it didn't necessarily say it was romantic, did it? Things like 'Soon.' 'I miss you.' 'Can't wait to be with you again.' 'I'll always love you.' Those are endearments and words that anticipate a person seeing a loved one again, but it doesn't have to be romantically."

That gave Wilder some semblance of hope. If this person didn't want Cosette romantically, then maybe he hadn't touched her…hurt her. His stomach curdled.

Roger stared at the board, studying theories and possible connections the team had scribbled. He rubbed his chin, then tapped it with his index finger. "Cosette had been a social worker while finishing up her doctorate in New Orleans, mainly with children, right?"

"Yes. That's why we focused on Washington, DC, patients. They were mostly adults and young adults. Why?"

"What if we can't find the culprit because we're not looking at the children? Children who would be young adults today."

"Why would a child from a decade or more ago want to kidnap Cosette? Or kill her?" Wilder asked.

"Maybe at first they didn't. At first, it was a fixated fantasy, but it didn't go like the vivid dream in their mind. Many times, it's very common for a young patient to transfer maternal feelings onto their therapist. These can be good feelings or bad. If Cosette worked with a child that had been abused or neglected, and was caring and kind to this child, then he or she could have wished for a mom like her…therefore, Cosette became their mom."

"You mean they wanted her to be their mom, but knew she wasn't, right?"

"At first. It's possible. But if this child fixated, dreamed…became delusional due to a break in reality, then it's very possible that they believe Cosette is indeed their mother."

"You said good feelings or bad. How do we know what's what? What do you mean?" Wilder wasn't sure where this was going, but he'd follow any rabbit trail that showed itself.

Roger exhaled. "If the child hated the mother, then those bad feelings would surface and it would be difficult for Cosette to have had any success in her sessions. She might have even been threatened. But because she was given gifts and positive notes at the beginning of this, I believe at the time of their therapy, it was a good maternal transference—if this theory proves to be right."

They didn't have any other theories. They'd work this one and see if it led anywhere. Wilder rubbed the back of his neck. "You think a patient of hers from her past might have had this maternal transference and came back now to do what?"

Roger perched on the edge of the desk as if he were teaching a psychology class. "Could be to reconnect. But like I said, it didn't go as the fantasy played out in their head and it turned aggressive."

"So we have a psycho on the loose." Great.

"Psychosis is a symptom of something. Not an actual diagnosis. The abductor may indeed be psychotic—had a break from reality. But my guess is that symptom is surfacing from someone who suffers from antisocial disorder. A former patient who's dreamed about their mom for a very long time."

Scrubbing his face, Wilder sighed. "How does one get this disorder?"

Roger cocked his head. "You can be born with it. Or develop it from experiencing neglect and abuse at a young age. Or it can be a mix of both. People with this disorder will have no remorse. As children, they'd exhibit disruptive behaviors, no impulse control, and as they grew it would develop into sociopathy. They would be masters of deception and manipulation."

That tracked with their suspicions about her patients being manipulated and deceived into trying to harm Cosette. "What happens if she tries to explain she's not Mommy Dearest?"

"For her safety, she's smart enough to go along with the break in reality. You can't reason with someone like that. Someone delusional." Roger scanned the room. "This person is highly calculating. No empathy. Unable to rationalize, as they've reverted back to the age of their trauma, and yet, incredibly, they can function in society as adults. It's complex, intriguing."

Roger seemed entirely too thrilled. This wasn't a research project.

"So what do we do, Renfrow?"

"Let's narrow the patient search to children with abusive and neglectful mothers. Prepubescent. New Orleans cases."

Wilder balled his fist. He didn't care if he was dealing with an adult with a warped child brain. He didn't even fully understand it. Whoever had Cosette was off their rocker and could kill her with a change in the wind.

TEN

"Hello, Mommy."

Unable to speak or breathe, Cosette lay on the princess-pink bed, paralyzed, stunned.

"Have you missed me?" She carried a tray with peanut butter crackers and soda in teacups. "I missed you. I've been stuck with those stupid people for so long. They adopted me and called me their daughter. But I know who I really belong to. The minute I turned eighteen, I came to look for you. To be with you. And now we're together again."

Her voice sounded like that of a small child. Her dark eyes were staring right through Cosette, vacant and glazed. She set the tray on the nightstand and walked to the dresser, then opened the jewelry box and wound the ballerina around until the tune "Somewhere My Love" started playing.

Cosette found her voice. "Did you send me that video of my music box? Is that the one from my apartment?"

"I know I'm not s'posed to go in your room and play with your things or your makeup, but I just had to!" She grinned. "Aren't you glad to be home, Mommy?"

"You drew on my mirror with the lipstick. Tried on my things and hid in my closet because you were afraid I'd get mad at you?" The intruder in her apartment hadn't knocked her down to be mean, but to escape punishment. *God, help me! Please!*

"Are you mad, Mommy? Because I'm a good girl. You know I am."

Those last words unlocked the past, and it rushed in like a wind. Cosette held back tears and whispered, "No, I'm not mad."

She'd been sent here over a decade ago to assess and counsel an eight-year-old little girl. She'd bonded with her over the jewelry box.

"Hi, I'm Miss Cosette."

The little girl cowered, a thumb in her mouth.

"It's okay. I'm here to help you." She studied the room. All done in princess pink. Eyeing the jewelry box, Cosette walked to it and opened it. "I had one just like this when I was a little girl."

"My mama gave me that. But she's dead."

Cosette's heart broke like it always did for the neglected, abused and lost. "I'm very sorry. Would you like to color?" The child might tell her more through drawings than speaking.

She nodded.

Cosette sat with her at the table coloring. "Can you draw me a picture of your happiest time?"

The child beamed and went to task.

"My mommy bought us a puppy. She loves puppies and I do, too." She colored it yellow.

"Where is your puppy now?"

"Dead." She scowled and broke her crayon. "Dead like Mommy."

"Do you want to talk about your mommy?" Cosette picked up a red crayon and drew a heart.

"I like your lipstick. It's red. I like red." She pointed to the heart on the paper. "I like hearts, too."

Cosette smiled and studied her a little longer. She wasn't exhibiting grief as expected for a child who'd witnessed her mother using a hair dryer in the bathtub to kill herself.

The little girl drew another picture. A woman with blond curly hair. A child with dark hair—herself—and a man with the face of a monster. "Who's that?"

"Mommy's boyfriend. She has lots of them. She doesn't like me when they're around. Sometimes she locks me in closets. That's mean. She got what she deserved!"

Neglect had been in the report. Her mother had suffered from depression. Diagnosed bipolar. Calls had been made before. Now she'd go to a foster home.

Cosette had counseled her three times. The child exhibited signs of antisocial disorder, so Cosette had requested the case manager do further psyche evals. She hadn't seen her again.

Not until five months ago, when the girl had started dating Wheezer.

Except Cosette hadn't recognized her then.

"Did you hear me, Mommy? Would you rather have ice cream instead of crackers?"

"Yes, Amy. I would." Swallowing down fear, Cosette gained control and reminded herself to stay calm and collected. She couldn't reason with Amy. The young woman was irrational, and agitating her could get Cosette killed. If she could get downstairs to the kitchen, then she could find a way to escape and get help. "Amy, did you leave those earrings for me at my mommy's grave?"

"I knew you would like them. Remember them? I gave them to you for Mother's Day. You took me to the fair to celebrate."

Amy may have purchased a cheaper pair as a child and her biological mom then took her to the fair—one of the better memories of her real mother.

"Tell me about the family that adopted you." Had she hurt them?

"I hate them! They kept me from you and I don't want to talk about them."

Amy opened the bedroom door with no fear of Cosette running away. In Amy's mind, her former therapist was her beloved mom and this was their home.

How had Cosette not seen the signs in the last five months she'd been around the woman? Because Amy was good. She'd hidden everything so well. From everyone. But it was Cosette's job to recognize the signs. Amy had always added in free pastries and took chances to be near her.

"Did you get the job at Sufficient Grounds to be close to me?" Amy had said she'd been searching for Cosette since she was eighteen. Now she was twenty. How long had she stalked Cosette? Watched. Plotted.

"I did. But your mean old boyfriend keeps cameras and I couldn't come over. So I found another way."

"Wheezer."

She'd expertly manipulated him and planted herself in Cosette's world. Coming and going. Wilder had given her free rein because he trusted Wheezer. Aurora trusted Amy. They all had.

Cosette followed Amy downstairs, the front door beckoning her to make a run through it. If she shoved Amy hard enough, she could sprint to a neighbor's house. Wait… The fuzziness in her head must have fogged her thoughts. Whose house was this now and where was the family? She'd been here more than a few hours, that was for sure.

Cries and grunts sounded from the kitchen. A woman? Children?

Oh, dear God, please don't let there be hurt hostages.

A shiver rippled down her back. "Amy, do we have guests?"

Amy turned, her dark eyes reflecting pure hatred. A wicked grin distorted her features. This young woman wasn't the coffee barista she'd come to know or the loving girlfriend Wheezer cared deeply for. She was a homicidal sociopath. As Cosette had feared the little girl would become when she'd counseled her as a child.

Placing her index finger on her mouth, Amy paused midstep. "Shh…they don't matter. They'll get what they deserve for being in our house."

Cosette glanced at the front door again. This changed things. If she made a run for it, innocent lives could end. The kind of rage Amy would exhibit might be fatal to everyone. Hope deflated as Cosette stepped into the sunny yellow kitchen with white cabinets and homemade art on the fridge. The puppy she'd rejected bounded toward her, jumping up on her legs.

Amy scooped him up. "She doesn't love you, pooch. But I do." She kissed him and let him down. Cries came from beyond the kitchen.

"Do you want vanilla or chocolate?" Amy asked.

Tiptoeing around the island, Cosette spotted the laundry room. "Whatever you like best," she said and craned her neck.

Sitting in a huddle were a woman, two elementary-aged children, a teenager and, lying on the floor in a pool of blood, a man. Amy had taken an entire family hostage.

Ice ran down Cosette's back and into her feet, freezing her like a stone statue. No wonder Amy was letting her roam free; she'd calculated this. And she was right. Cosette would never leave them. She had to find a way to free them and help the wounded man. The children—

all precious blonde girls. The horror etched on their little faces made Cosette want to vomit.

"Amy," she said in a shaky voice. "That man in there is hurt really bad. I need to check on him. Make sure he's alive. Can I do that?"

"Why do you care about that man? Is he another boy-friend?" Her eyes darkened. "You always care about boy-friends over me." Anger was simmering in her voice, and if Cosette didn't play this right it would boil over and scald them all.

"I don't care about that man." *Think fast.* "I care about you. If he dies, Amy, then you could go to jail and we'll never be together. You don't want that, do you?"

She seemed to think about it. "Fine, but if you so much as do anything bad, Mommy… I'll punish you. Just like I had to punish you before."

Cosette's mouth turned dry. "Tell me what I did, Amy. What did I do to deserve punishment?" She slowly made her way toward the laundry room.

"You know what you did! I don't like doing bad things to you, but you make me! You make me do it."

The warning sounded like echoed words from Amy's mentally ill mother. Cossette had heard this from children before, but right now was having a hard time finding sympathy for the young woman who'd "punished" her. She had to mean the muffins with nut products and running her down, whether it was Amy herself or Ka-riss. Now was not the time to ask that. Right now a man's life was at stake, along with his family's. She couldn't let them watch him die before their eyes.

"I won't be a bad mommy." She slipped into the laundry room.

The mother's hands were bound behind her back, like her children's, and tied to the louvered laundry doors;

their mouths were gagged and their feet were bound. The woman threw her body in front of her children and screamed through the gag.

Cosette's eyes filled with moisture and she held out her hands in a sign of surrender as she squatted, then motioned for her to be quiet. "It's okay," she whispered. "My name is Cosette LaCroix. I'm a psychologist and I'm going to get us out of here."

The question was how? Amy was diabolical. Homicidal. Unhinged.

"I want to check your husband's vitals. I won't hurt any of you, I promise. I'm going to help." Again, she had no clue how.

The woman nodded frantically, eyes bugging out of her head as tears streaked down her cheeks.

"I can't take off your gag. It might produce behavior none of us want. Do you understand?" She didn't want the children to hear that Amy might murder them all if she thought Cosette was being a bad mom.

The children had tearstains on their faces. Eyes wide with fright, they shivered uncontrollably. They were in shock. Not good. The youngest had had an accident in her pants. *God, cradle her right now. Cradle us all.* "Be brave. We'll get through this," Cosette whispered and checked the man's pulse.

Slow. Faint.

But alive.

He'd been shot, but hadn't bled out yet, which meant he'd been shot recently—maybe he'd tried to free his family and escape. It also meant Amy had a gun.

That was another game changer. "Amy, this man could die if we don't get him medical attention. You don't want that, do you?"

She entered the laundry room.

The woman and her girls flinched.

Amy shifted on her feet and tucked the corner of her bottom lip between her teeth, cocking her head. Like a small child unsure of how to answer. "He got what he deserved. He tried to keep me from my house!" Child-like eyes narrowed into a killer's and her voice shifted back to a young woman's, only with a hard, cold edge. "And if he dies then so what?" She stomped back into the kitchen and hollered, "Your ice cream is gonna melt. You asked for it. You better eat every bite."

What to do? If Cosette didn't cooperate, they all could die. If she walked away from this family, a husband and father would lose his life. The woman's eyes filled with tears. She knew the reality of the situation. That her husband was going to die in front of them all. And possibly her children, too.

Cosette held back burning tears. Her own terror and uncertainty wouldn't benefit anyone. It might set Amy off. The man needed pressure applied to his gunshot wound.

Cosette was trapped.

She grabbed a towel off the dryer and applied it to the wound near his shoulder, praying the bullet hadn't hit something important. Even if it hadn't, he'd lost so much blood. Spotting clothespins on the dryer, she snatched them and worked to make a tight tourniquet, sealing it with the wooden pins. Then she laid the woman's legs over it to help with pressure. It wasn't great, but it was all she could come up with.

"Mommy!" Amy screeched at an ear-piercing level. "Get. In. Here!"

"I'm sorry," Cosette said with a strangled cry. "I'm so sorry. I'll be back as soon as I can." She hurried into the kitchen and washed the blood from her hands, watching through blurry eyes as it swirled red down the drain. Then she approached the table, where her bowl of vanilla ice cream awaited. How was she supposed to force the cold treat down when she was riddled with nausea?

Easing into her chair, she glanced at Amy, who had no problem wolfing down a bowl of chocolate ice cream. Amy looked up and paused, then grabbed a backpack and handed it over. "Look inside."

Cosette unzipped the bag with trembling fingers. Inside were several brochures and an itinerary. "It's our summer vacation. Doesn't it look fun?"

"Do you have any big plans with Wheezer this summer?"

"No, I'm spending it with my mom."

That's what she'd said that first morning in the coffee shop, when Cosette had received the note that a present awaited her at her mother's grave. She'd meant Cosette. Amy'd had a lovesick look in her eyes, which Cosette thought was over Wheezer, but Amy had been dreaming of being reunited with her mom, aka Cosette.

Blood drained from Cosette's face. She felt faint.

"Say you like it."

She forced herself to reply. "I like it," she muttered. "But I'd really like it if we could help that man in there. That would…that would make Mommy happy. You want to make Mommy happy, don't you?"

Amy's eyes widened and she jumped up, slinging her bowl across the room. It shattered into tiny shards across the floor. The mother and girls in the laundry room began to sob again.

Pointing her spoon at Cosette, Amy leaned forward. "I have tried to make you happy! I got us tickets to your favorite movie and when I showed up, guess who was sitting in my seat? Your boyfriend. I gave you your favorite muffin, and you know what? You gave it to your boyfriend!"

"I'm allergic to nuts, Amy."

"I know that! Now. Aurora told me you were deathly allergic and kept an EpiPen. But that's not the point—you still gave it to him. To. Him!"

When Amy had asked what was in the muffin box, it had been for show. She knew because she'd planted them. The call! It had come from Amy. She'd been in the kitchen making it. Right there at CCM!

"I bought you a puppy and you refused it. You'd rather have horses with your *boyfriend*! Nothing makes you happy!" She wailed and pulled at her hair, stomping on the floor. "And you took that other girl to the park!"

Her punishments for the perceived rejection and neglect: the box of muffins with nut products. Burning down the stable. Running her over and targeting not only her, but Renny, and clipping Jody in the hip. "Amy, was that you in Kariss's car or did Kariss punish me?"

"Eat your ice cream," she screamed at bloodcurdling levels, then stormed into the laundry room, pulling a gun with a suppressor from her waistband. "Mommy says I should help you. But I think you all deserve to die!"

Wilder shoved away the sandwich his sister laid on his desk. "I don't want to eat."

"And if you don't, you'll lose strength and be good to no one. Now, shove it down, soldier!" Caley placed her hands on her hips.

"You look and sound just like Ma." He half laughed—the first time since Cosette had been missing. Almost three days.

They'd combed files, hacked mainframes, made calls. Everyone worked around the clock. They'd narrowed down about sixty-two patients that fitted the bill. Roger Renfrow sat in the conference room with Dr. McMillian this very moment going through them, profiling and making phone calls. Wilder probably owed them both an apology for threatening them. Every now and then, Roger's coughs would echo through the house. A lonely house when it was void of Cosette.

Caley pointed at the coffee. "Drink it. I know you haven't slept. Just because you're trained to go without sleep doesn't mean you should. Y'all are in this together and everyone is equally capable of doing the work. Rest, Wilder. At least an hour or two."

"I'll rest when I find her. That's that, Caley."

"Well, at least shave!" She spun and stormed from the room.

He rubbed the three day's growth on his face. Felt the dryness of his eyes. He'd squirt some drops to help clear the bloodshot look. He had managed a quick shower every day. His sister should be thankful for that.

Beckett knocked and stepped inside. Wilder saw his expression and knew this conversation wasn't going to be about Cosette. Beckett hadn't said anything about Meghan since Wilder revealed the truth. He deserved a major butt kicking. He'd take it like a man, too.

Beckett sank into the chair across the desk, his hair disheveled. "I'm not angry that you found her first. I'm not angry that your words were the last words she heard." He cleared his throat and his nostrils flared. Talking about Meghan would never be easy for any of them. "I don't even think if you had told me the truth at the time, I'd have let you take the blame. I believed it was all my fault. Even when you said it wasn't."

Wilder understood implicitly.

"I get why you felt you couldn't share that with me or

anyone. We're stubborn men. Gotta carry it all for everyone, and you did, Wilder. You carried me through that whole nightmare and refused to let me fall into an abyss. But it wasn't your sole responsibility. It was God's."

Wilder swallowed hard. "Where is God right now, Beck? I don't feel Him at all. I prayed. I asked forgiveness. I'm playing it by the good book. He knows where she is. Why can't He just tell us somehow? Send us a message. We have nothing other than sixty-two leads. Do you know how long it could be before we narrow it down to a handful? And by then…" His voice cracked. It was too hard to go there.

"Good behavior doesn't dictate what God will or won't do. He's all about grace and mercy. Not works. And just because you don't feel Him or see Him doesn't mean He isn't working on your behalf." Beckett stood. "I just wanted you to know that I'm not mad at you for that night." He inhaled, rubbed his jaw. "Did she…did she say anything? Was she…in pain?"

Wilder would spare Beckett. "She didn't say anything and she went quickly."

Beck nodded once. "I'm glad she didn't go alone, you know. That you were there. That was God's mercy. His grace."

The back of Wilder's eyes burned and a knot formed in his throat.

"I'll check in on the doctors and see what we have." Beckett quietly left the room.

Now what?

I know good behavior doesn't force Your hand or get me what I want. So how about some mercy? Please have mercy, God.

Cosette's phone rang in her purse. That blasted lawyer. What could he possibly want? Wilder's gut told him to answer. Cosette would be fit to be tied, but he hit the green button. "Hello."

"Who is this?"

"This is Wilder Flynn. Cosette works for me at Covenant Crisis Management. I think she's made it pretty clear that she doesn't want anything to do with your client. I'm only answering because it seems you aren't good at taking hints. The hint being she won't reply."

Leon LaCroix's lawyer sighed. "I understand. But Leon won't let up on me calling."

"You'd think when she didn't set up a payment system with the prison for collect calls to her cell phone that would have given him a clue."

"Well, I couldn't send her a letter. I didn't have an address. What choice did I have? I work for my client. Would you ask her to please speak with me? I have information that she might need to hear."

This perked Wilder's attention. "What kind of information? Cosette isn't here at the moment."

"She conveniently left you her phone?" Doubt laced his words.

"I assure you it wasn't convenient. But I'm as good as you're going to get, Mr...?"

"Broland."

One beat passed.

Two.

"Mr. LaCroix informed me that someone came to see him in January. A woman."

"And?"

"She said she was a close friend of Cosette's, showed him some recent photos. Seemed believable."

"But?"

"It wasn't until a few days after she visited, and his excitement that Cosette might be willing to come and see him—even forgive him—dissipated, that he thought the encounter was strange and felt a need to contact his daughter about it."

"What was odd about the visit?" And who was this mystery woman?

"She initially started with letting him know that she was coming to see if Leon was worthy of Cosette's forgiveness—which is odd right there, in my opinion. Cosette has shown no interest in contacting her father, let alone forgiving him for what transpired."

Transpired? The man had murdered Cosette's mother in a drunken rage, so that wasn't the word Wilder would use. But that did sound odd. "Why didn't that alone raise a red flag with him?"

"Because he's desperate for Cosette's forgiveness. He wasn't thinking clearly. He just emptied himself out to this woman. He told her how he'd become a Christian, was sober. What would you have done?"

Wilder wasn't sure. Good for Leon, if he truly had found faith in Jesus while in prison. And he had no choice but to be sober. "Is that all? You've been hounding Cosette for five months over this?" Wilder might have done the same thing. What was this woman's motive for visiting Leon LaCroix?

"No. She not only shared stories of her and Cosette, but she peppered him with questions. At the time, they seemed innocent enough. Subtle. But as I said before—it nagged at Leon. He felt Cosette might be in some kind of trouble or danger."

Daddy LaCroix wasn't off base. "Anything else?"

Papers rustled over the line. "She mentioned she and Cosette were taking a summer trip."

"Where?" This could be where she'd been taken.

"Something about a cruise out of New Orleans."

"Date?"

"Early June. She mentioned Cozumel."

What in the world? Wilder scratched his head. "These innocent questions. Did he reveal them to you?"

"He did. The one that stuck out most was about Cosette's mother and where she was buried."

"Did he answer them?"

"Yes. And then he got worried and called me. He wanted to confirm that Kristy was her friend—"

A name! "Kristy who?"

"Tabor."

"He give you a description of the woman?" Didn't matter, Wilder would get it from the camera feed at the prison.

"Dark hair. Dark eyes. Pretty. Slender. Maybe five foot five."

"Ballpark age?"

"Early twenties."

Now to decide what to tell this guy about Cosette. "Someone has been stalking Cosette recently. Since January. It could be this woman. Thank you for calling. This is helpful."

"But she's okay? Leon will want to know."

Wilder wrestled with what to say and decided on the truth. "Actually, she's been abducted. We're doing everything we can to find her. Tell him this information could be useful. That he's helped us. I'll call the prison and get Kristy's address and phone number and the footage."

Finally, a lead. He hung up and rushed into the control room. Wheezer and Evan raised their heads. Jody stood at the whiteboard working to connect dots.

"I need everything you can find on a Kristy Tabor, and all cruises leaving from New Orleans the first three weeks in June. And if you can get savvy, I want a manifest with Cosette's name and/or Kristy Tabor's. I need it yesterday."

He blew from there into the conference room. The doctors stopped talking. "Anyone in those files by the name of Kristy Tabor? She'd be in her early twenties now. Dark hair. Dark eyes. Seen anyone like that at the clinic? She's clearly been lurking."

Roger flipped through a few folders. "Tabor sounds familiar. I think I may have come across that name. Let me look back over the files."

Now to call the prison in New Orleans and request that footage. If he played it right, they might email it over and save some time.

An hour later, Roger Renfrow held up a file. "Okay. Tabor is the maiden name of a woman who committed suicide. Her daughter was eight."

"Name of daughter?"

"Amy Neilson. Ring a bell?"

Wilder frowned. "Amy Neilson...no."

Five feet five. Dark hair. Dark eyes. Early twenties. The only Amy he knew...

Wheezer, Jody and Evan entered the conference room; Wheezer's face had turned ghostly white. He was shaking his head.

Evan glanced at his colleague, patted his shoulder, then took the lead. "We found one ship. Carnival. Leaving port June 17. But there is no Kristy Tabor. However, there is a Cosette LaCroix and she's registered with—" he glanced again at Wheezer "—Amy Payne."

Amy Payne!

She must have been adopted. "Wheezer, where is Amy?"

He shook his head, still didn't speak.

"I'm sorry, man, really, but we'll have to deal with this

later," Wilder stated. "Now we need to find Cosette." At least if a cruise was booked, she planned to keep Cosette alive, which gave him some comfort. He trusted Cosette would use her professional skills to survive but the flip side of the coin was that Amy was unhinged and anything could go wrong at any point in time.

"I told her about Beau Chauvert manhandling Cosette. She was here all the time. She'd easily have known about the dark web and the anonymous software. I basically gave her a tutorial on it because she was interested in the case—but she was simply learning how to navigate under the radar. That's why we couldn't trace the jewelry box email." Wheezer was clearly stupefied. "She could have easily stolen Frank's ball cap. She'd know where he ate every day," Wheezer added. "This is all my fault."

"Sweetie, let's not play the blame game again," Jody said. "The girl fooled us all. Played us all. Could easily have stalked and befriended Kariss Elroy and Malcolm Hayes—got Malcolm to torch the stable wearing those clothes, and she may have asked to borrow Kariss's car. Not sure where Jeffrey Levitts comes into play, but who knows... So ease up on yourself, okay?" She rubbed Wheezer's back and gave him a squeeze.

"If she's boarding a cruise ship, she's in New Orleans," Wilder said.

Aurora had come in with fresh coffee and pursed her lips and shook her head. "She asked for the summer off. To take a vacation with her mother. She meant Cosette!"

Wheezer grabbed a fistful of his coppery-blond hair. "She was on her way over. I told her to wait because the police were here, taking Cosette, and I might have work to do. She said that was fine, because her mother came into town early and they were going to be gone for a few days. I guess she had to think fast and grab Cosette now, so she lied to me. Amy must have planned to hold Cosette somewhere until time for the summer cruise." He slumped into a chair. Wilder understood that kind of guilt. But Wheezer couldn't have known. This wasn't his fault.

"Well, wouldn't you have wondered what happened when she didn't show up in a few days?" Evan asked.

"She had accomplished her mission. Taken Cosette. I would be a moot point. All of us." Wheezer held his head in his hands.

"It's gonna be okay, Wheezer," Wilder said. He just wasn't sure how yet.

"If she's living in the past, she might take Cosette to the place it all began," Dr. McMillian offered. "Amy's childhood home."

Roger agreed. "I have the address of the house in New Orleans."

Wilder bit down on his bottom lip, thinking. He could be there in an hour and a half, direct flight, but he'd want weapons. Not just one. Senator Townes owed him a favor; they'd saved his life not long ago during a shooting at a rally. He owned a private jet. But a lot could happen in an hour.

"You considering going alone or calling in NOPD?" Shep asked. "You know what I would do."

When Caley had been abducted, Shep chose himself over the police department. He had special ops training. So did Wilder. "If I call them, I'll have SWAT to deal with, and everyone knows they'd rather pull a trigger and call it a day rather than sit for hours in position while someone tries to negotiate."

"Amy won't negotiate," Roger said. "She's not rational. She'd rather die *with* Cosette than see them torn apart again."

An hour and a half of waiting might kill him.

"Carrington Jones!" Wilder and Beckett said in unison.

Carrington was a private investigator in New Orleans. And Teddy's twin sister. They'd been in the private eye business together until she married and moved to Louisiana.

Beckett grinned. "Great minds think alike."

"I'll give her a call. Tell her the situation and have her put eyes on the house. See if Cosette is inside. Safe. If not, I trust her to be swift." Carrington had been a navy girl, too. "Otherwise, she sits on the house until we arrive." He grabbed his cell and called Senator Townes.

Wilder would take every shot that came his way. Even if it was in the dark.

ELEVEN

"No! Don't!"

Amy pulled the trigger.

Cosette was too late.

The poor man was dead. He'd done nothing to deserve it. His family was sobbing, screaming through the gags. Cosette's lips quivered.

Amy swung the gun around. "You care more about them than me. If they're dead, you have no one to think about *but* me."

"Amy, please!" Cosette held her hands up. "Don't kill them..." *Think fast.* "I'm sorry. You're right. I'm not focused on you like I should be. Can you forgive me? Please say you can...daughter." The words tasted sour, but she had to keep this woman and her children alive. They'd need counseling for decades after witnessing this. Blood throbbed in Cosette's ears.

Toying with the gun, Amy cocked her head, then grinned. "I forgive you. Now let's go upstairs and pack for our cruise."

Cosette couldn't leave this man lying like this. The sobs and screams were enough to make her faint. "Amy," she said, as demurely as she could, "I think it might make them sad to see their daddy like this. Why don't we move him?" *God, help me!* Worst case scenario, but the small children...she had to do something.

Eyes like a shark's stared back at her. It was a long shot, trying to force a sociopath to feel empathy. And she couldn't mention what it made Amy feel like to witness her mother's suicide. She had felt nothing.

"I want to pack. Let's pack." Amy put the puppy in his kennel and motioned with the gun for her to go. Cosette caught the woman's eye. Defeat. Hopelessness. Stark terror. Mouthing that she was sorry, which felt weak at best, she headed upstairs, Amy behind her with the gun. To pack.

"I took some of your clothes from your apartment. Why did you move in with your boyfriend? He doesn't love you. *I* love you."

Cosette chose her words carefully and studied the array of clothing in the master bedroom. Items lying across a bed the poor wife would have to sleep in alone— if she didn't move away, or die, first. "I was afraid of Jeffrey Levitts." She left out that they'd thought he was stalking her. Amy would consider all she'd done as gifts and favors. Stalking would be a negative term, and angering Amy was something Cosette couldn't afford to do.

"Do you know he thought you wanted him? Eww. He's old."

"How do you know that?" she asked, as nonchalantly as possible and folded a pair of shorts, then placed them in the suitcase to placate Amy.

"Because when Wheezer told me what he'd done to you and that he'd once been your boyfriend, I knew, and it made me mad. Just like what that mean man did to you at your reunion. Wheezer told me that, too."

"Amy, did you punish that bad man from my reunion? You can tell Mommy. I won't be mad." Cosette gripped a shirt and squeezed.

She nodded, as if she was proud of murdering him. "I did. I drove all night when I found out that he hurt you. And I made him pay."

She'd beaten him to a bloody pulp. Cosette managed not to cringe.

"And mean old Jeffrey Levitts? Did you make him pay?"

Amy plopped in the chair by the bed and picked up a book that had been lying on the table beside it. A Harlequin romance with a heroic cowboy cover. Cosette needed her hero right now. On a horse. A motorcycle. A trike, for all she cared. Wilder was tracking her down, she had no doubt. But would it be in time? Would he have any idea to search for a woman?

"I sent him an email using that software. Remember that? Those guys used it to frame Evan."

Cosette nodded. Amy had all kinds of private information.

"He thought I was you. I asked him to meet me at Malcolm's."

"You know Malcolm?"

Amy folded her arms across her chest. "Don't act stupid! You know I know Malcolm. How do you think those tickets and gift card got into your office? I watched him for days and he was so easy to become friends with. I'm not unattractive."

She'd stalked him. All this time Cosette thought Jeffrey had the power to do this, but so did Amy and she had.

Poor Malcolm. Cosette had never once suspected him. But when she'd turned her back to retrieve his file, he easily could have placed the envelope there, and he'd been agitated that day. He might not have wanted to do it. Or he was afraid of getting caught. She'd assumed the agitation and panic was from his struggle with wanting to start a fire and knowing he shouldn't.

"He was an idiot. All I had to do was say 'fire' and he was at my beck and call. I gave him that hat and clothing and had him burn that stable down. He should have killed your boyfriend. Had I known he'd be in there, I'd have done it myself. Watched him die." Her smile turned sinister. Sadistic. "Jeffrey thought he was meeting you at Malcolm's. Malcolm thought we were meeting someone who could help him stop burning up things. He felt so bad about it. Big deal." She snorted.

Amy had made it look like a murder-suicide.

"Did you punish Kariss?"

"Kariss was my friend, just like Malcolm was. Until she told me no. She didn't want to give you those muffins. She was afraid I'd done something bad. But she was weak. Stupid. Sometimes, she let me borrow her car." Amy giggled with delight, as if it was a secret that she'd been the one to try and run them down, kill them.

Another staged suicide.

Cosette continued packing.

When they were done, Amy forced her to watch an old movie. And she finally agreed to give the hostages a bathroom break, but wouldn't let Cosette take them, instead making her stand at the door where Amy could see every move she made.

"Could we give them some water?"

"No!"

They were already showing signs of dehydration. It had been almost three days according to the calendar on the refrigerator. They could die. But Cosette didn't press the issue. Dehydration was better than death...though not far from it.

A knock on the front door startled her.

Amy scowled. "Don't any of you move." She aimed the gun at the youngest girl. "You so much as breathe loud and she gets one to the head."

They stood silently in the laundry room.

The doorbell rang.

"If you don't go see about it, whoever it is might call the police. Do you want the cops here? They'll ruin our trip." If Cosette could get Amy to the door, she might have a chance to free the hostages, or at the very least, sneak the little ones some water. "Neighbors are nosy. Go put it to rest."

Growling, Amy stomped through the kitchen, and Cosette knelt and grabbed the ties that bound the woman to the louvered laundry doors. She grunted and used her head to point to her children.

Get them out first. Of course. That was a real mother's love. Sacrifice.

Cosette worked on untying the teenage girl as Amy chatted with a woman at the front door. *Keep her talking, lady. Keep her talking.* The harder she tried to undo the knots, the more Cosette fumbled. Finally, she got the teen's hands free. The girl ungagged herself and went to work untying her ankles, while Cosette quietly worked to release one of the younger children. Then together they untied the other one.

Freedom!

"Go out the side door and get help. Tell them to call the police, and Wilder Flynn in Atlanta. Can you remember that?" Cosette said as she worked on the mom's ties. They were tighter. Stronger.

They'd been traumatized and might forget. But the teen nodded frantically.

"Mommy!"

Amy was coming!

The girl's eyes widened and one of her sisters cried. The teen herded them out the side door to the backyard. No time to finish untying the mom. Cosette had to stall Amy. Give the girls a fighting chance.

When Amy discovered they'd gotten loose, that Cosette had done it…she didn't want to think about the consequences. Not for her. Not for the woman sitting on the floor staring at the door, her best chance at freedom, her hope that her children would live.

Cosette hurried from the laundry room into the kitchen. "Who was it?"

"A neighbor. Don't I look like a good house sitter? I told her the Carsons had to go out of town. Family emergency." She held up brownies. "Apparently, Mrs. Jones bakes the kids treats from time to time. Said I could keep them and the kids could eat them when they get home." She carried them to the kitchen counter. "They look store-bought to me. Whatever. You want one?"

"No, thank you. I remembered I might get cold on the cruise. That night air. I didn't pack a hoodie. Did you? Let's go check. I don't want you to catch a cold."

Amy studied her. Could she hear her heart pounding? See the lies in her eyes?

She pulled the gun, pointed it at Cosette. "In the laundry room. Now."

No!

Amy saw the girls were missing, then glanced out the open door.

They were trying to unlock the back gate. One was climbing up the six-foot fence.

No!

Amy's face turned two shades of red. "How. Dare. You!" She lunged forward.

Cosette raised her hand to protect herself. "Amy, don't!" Fear drew her fist back to fight, but Amy was too quick.

The butt of the gun came down on her head.

Wilder and his team had flown in to New Orleans just as day gave way to night.

They met Carrington down the street from Amy's childhood home. Her hair was longer, blonder. She didn't bother with greetings or niceties. He admired that about her. All business. She'd called Wilder while they were on the plane and left a message to let him know she'd done a search on the address.

Family of five. Where were they? Dread pooled in Wilder's gut. He hoped they were out of town.

After gathering necessary information, Carrington had delivered brownies to the house. Amy had answered. Carrington didn't see Cosette or the family, but the car parked in the drive was registered to the man of the house. According to her, nothing seemed out of place or disturbed. Amy didn't seem terribly agitated.

But the PI hadn't been able to see that Cosette was safe, and that made Wilder nervous. What if he was too late? He needed to get to her *now*. He needed…some help. His team had rallied around him. Aided him. But even so, he was calling the shots. Making the moves. Carving out the paths.

A verse from Proverbs that Wilder had learned at a young age came to mind: *Trust in the Lord with all thine heart; and lean not unto thine own understanding. In all thy ways acknowledge Him, and He shall direct thy paths.*

He'd been relying on himself for so long. Leaning on his own understanding—his military training, life experience, books—but he'd never truly relied on God. Not as a child. Not as someone who needed guidance. He'd thought he'd been guiding himself pretty well. But that wasn't true.

He'd acknowledged God as his heavenly Father. Acknowledged Jesus as his Savior, but then Wilder had drawn the line. He didn't even know when it had happened. It had been a slow fade. *Lord, forgive me. I can't do this alone. I'm a mess. Please direct our paths.*

All these years, he'd chalked up his gut feelings to a sixth sense of sorts. But the truth was it had been the guidance of the Lord. The gift of discernment that came from God. *Please forgive me. I haven't even acknowledged all the times You've led me safely through missions. All the times You've guided my hand at my job. In my life. I've given myself the glory. Lord, I'm sorry.*

He'd prayed days earlier, but the truth was he'd done it because he was supposed to. He hadn't really felt it. Not until now. Peace settled over him. Calmed his jumpy nerves. When was the last time he'd felt this kind of peace? He didn't even know. Renewed strength came in a burst. No longer was he carrying everyone. God was carrying them all, Wilder included.

"…and other than that, nothing new since we last talked," Carrington said and squeezed into the back seat of their rental SUV. "Blinds are all closed. It's been quiet. Game plan?" she asked.

"In. Out. No one the wiser." That had been the plan in Istanbul, too, when Allie had died. But this time, Wilder wasn't looking to himself to control everything—to control life and death. He'd do his very best as a man and leave the rest to God.

"You want me to pray?" Beckett asked.

For once, Wilder would. He would acknowledge in his own voice who had this. It wasn't him. "I'll do it." He bowed his head and prayed for everyone's safety and no causalities. Everyone said *amen.*

"We go in small numbers. Stealth," Wilder said. They were trained to be invisible. If they didn't want to be seen, they wouldn't be. "Things go sideways, then we involve the police with all the lights and fanfare. But let's not need them until this is over and an arrest has to be made. We take Amy alive. No fatalities unless it's absolutely necessary."

Everyone agreed.

Only Wheezer remained quiet. He never came out for fieldwork, but he had a personal investment and Wilder couldn't deny him. Plus despite being stuck at a desk 24/7, he was a good shot—not that Wilder believed for a second he'd take the shot if he needed to.

"I'm going to make one pass, so everyone look fast and thoroughly." Wilder drove through the cove.

"All's quiet in the hood," Evan said. "Lights on in the house next door, but dim."

Beckett grunted. "Car in the drive. Just like you said, Carrington."

"No sign of movement inside," Shepherd noted.

"The light has gone on and off a few times in that window with the stained glass," Carrington murmured. "I assume it's a bathroom. It flicked on about ten minutes or so ago."

Wilder drove back down and two streets over, then parked on the side of the road.

"Jody, Evan, Wheezer. Take the back of the house. Beck and Carrington will go with me to the front. Shep, you keep an eye out in case she's in there and they run. Remember, we're shadows."

"Let's dance then," Shep muttered and they hustled like the wind, keeping to the dark, moving with speed and silence as they'd been trained. No one would see them coming.

Not even Amy.

Cold. So cold. Cosette shivered and gasped. Water seeped into her mouth. She opened her eyes. She was lying in a large bathtub as if she were about to take a luxury soak, only she was fully clothed, hands tied behind her back, feet bound and knotted to the faucet, which was running freezing cold water.

Panic sent her jolting and water splashed up her nose. She coughed and wriggled her hands, trying to free herself. Another streak of fear shot through her. Had Amy killed the remaining hostages? Cosette raised her chin and twisted against the ropes on her wrists, but kept slipping under the water, unable to get any traction with her feet, since they were out of the tub and bound. Was Amy going to drown her here?

She squeezed her eyes shut. Her shivers slowed as the cold water numbed her. This couldn't be how she'd die. Tears streaked her cheeks and she hiccupped. "I tried, God." She'd tried to save the family downstairs and failed. So many people dead because of her.

And now she was going to die.

Alone.

Wasn't that how she'd wanted it? A life alone. To belong to no one but herself. She'd built a hedge around her heart from Wilder. And now she'd gotten exactly what she wanted.

But it wasn't what she wanted at all, and she'd never get the chance to try and rectify it.

The words she'd slung at him now sliced at her.

That he was obsessive. Controlling. Intrusive.

But he was also relentless—just like Jody said. He was confident and a take-charge man, focused on the safety and protection of others. And he was intrusive because he cared. But he also knew how to give Cosette space. To acquiesce to the boundaries she'd placed on him.

Did it matter that he didn't share every little secret

in his past? She hadn't. She was a hypocrite, and there was no chance of her ever getting to make things right.

She'd die, and he'd live never knowing the truth.

That she loved him. No matter how hard she'd tried to convince herself that she didn't. That he'd end up hurting her. That he was like all the others. Still, she'd fallen for him.

And hurt him. Those words… She'd seen the look on his face. Known that she'd cut him.

She couldn't even ask for his forgiveness for that.

And she'd never forgiven her father. "God, forgive me." She should have. She should have bent her knee to the Lord and surrendered to what He'd asked of her. She'd been stubborn, willful, and in this moment, it all seemed so small.

Dad might never know it, but she could forgive him in her heart. Mom would understand. She was in heaven, where things were perfect. No pain. No regrets. No anger or sorrow. Just peace and happiness in the light of Jesus. Why hadn't Cosette seen it before?

Because she hadn't been about to die. She'd thought she had time. But time was short. "Dad," she cried and felt a warmth flow inside her, "I…forgive you."

Something like heavy jagged bricks lifted from her heart. She cried. She missed Mama—though she'd see her soon. But she also cried with relief. The tight, coiled ball of hatred and bitterness had been released and for once she felt like she could breathe. She hadn't even known she wasn't taking deep, full breaths. She'd been living with it so long it had become a part of her, the blame and lack of forgiveness.

Then she cried for Wilder. For all they could have been if they weren't so full of pride and fear. They claimed to be brave, but when the most important thing in the world was at stake—love—they were cowards. Both of them.

Amy entered the room, her dark eyes full of venom. She turned off the faucet. "You are a bad, bad mommy. And you're gonna get what you deserve."

She knelt and retrieved a hair dryer from under the sink.

Cosette's shivers resumed. Terror rattled her bones.

Amy plugged in the dryer.

She hadn't witnessed her mom's suicide.

At eight years old, she'd murdered her own mother. She was going to do it again. To Cosette.

"Amy, please. Think about this. We'll lose the cruise if you do this."

"I gave you plenty of chances to be a good mommy. I tried to make you love me. I thought you did. But you don't. You care more about those stupid people downstairs than you do me! Your own daughter!"

Cosette didn't dare inquire about the hostages. If they were alive, it could get them killed.

She was going to die at the hands of a homicidal sociopath who believed Cosette belonged to her. The irony coiled around her lungs and squeezed like a vise until she couldn't breathe. She'd been looking to Wilder to save her, protect her. But that was too much to put on him. He was just a man. She truly was alone, with no one to rely on but God, and she should have been looking to Him all along. If she'd run to God all those times she hurt, instead of to men who couldn't fill those empty places inside her—they only added to her scars—she might not be here. But she couldn't look back.

God, forgive me. I look to You to save me. Somehow. Some way. Save me. Fresh tears fell. *Because I know I don't belong to myself. I belong to You. I trust You. No matter what.*

"You should have known better! Why would you do that?"

"Amy, listen. It's just you and me. Please, don't do this."

"You never pay me attention. You want everybody but me. You're going to get what you deserve!" She turned on the hair dryer and hovered over the tub.

"Give me another chance, Amy," Cosette pleaded.

"I gave you chances!"

"Just one more!"

Suddenly, the door burst open. Cosette shrieked.

Amy held the hair dryer lower.

Wilder! *Thank You, God. Thank You for sending Wilder.* How had he found her? She'd thought all was lost. But here he was, dressed in black, gun aimed at Amy and fire in his eyes. "Cosette, you okay?"

She was in a tub full of cold water with a running hair dryer a foot away. No. She was not. "Yes."

"You!" Amy screamed. "I hate you. You always take her away from me. Well, nobody's gonna have her now."

"Amy…" Wheezer approached behind Wilder's shoulder. Slowly. Softly "You don't want to do this."

She threw her head back and laughed. "Look at you. All puppy-dog-eyed and hoping I'll do as you ask because I love you." She cackled again. "I don't love you."

Oh, Wheezer. Humiliation colored his cheeks.

Wilder tossed a glance to the electrical outlet and back to the hair dryer humming on full blast, as if to gauge whether he could unplug it in time.

No way. The second he moved, she'd drop it. The truth was in her eyes. There would be no negotiating. Wilder seemed to know it, judging by the look on his face. He glanced at Cosette and the dryer. His finger slowly moved toward the trigger, but he hesitated. He knew what Cosette did: that if he dropped Amy with a bullet, the dryer would land in the tub.

She was looking at the man she loved—a full beard, shaggy hair she adored—and this was where it was going to end.

Wilder would blame himself for her death.

Like he did Alan's... The fact suddenly dawned on her. And like he did Allie's—he must have had some part in that to feel responsible... And he couldn't bear to admit it out loud. That's why he refused therapy sessions. He didn't want to reveal what he'd consider weakness.

What would he hold on to in order to stay connected with her?

"Beck," Wilder whispered, "send the owl to the tower."

She didn't see Beckett, but knew he was there somewhere in the hallway. She also knew what that command meant. Wilder was sending Shepherd up on a roof with a sniper rifle as backup if things went south.

He said he'd go to whatever lengths necessary and he'd deem this necessary. It probably was, but Cosette had seen enough death. Too much blood. Too much loss.

She swallowed and inhaled deeply.

"Wilder, I want you to leave," Cosette said.

He kept his sight trained on Amy, but a brief cloud of confusion fogged his eyes. "No can do, darlin'."

"I'm not your darlin'," she snapped. This wasn't going to go well. So she'd say what she had to and hold it together the best she could. "I never said I needed to be rescued. You always think you have to try and save me." She glanced at Amy, who had the same cloud of confusion on her face. "You don't own me. I don't belong to you."

But she wanted to. To have his back. She already had, when she'd pulled him from the stable. And he had hers.

He grimaced.

Come on, Wilder. Please understand me.

"Do you not know me at all?" she asked.

That had his attention and he slowly slid a glance her way.

That's right, we say it all the time. But you do know me. Hear my heart.

"I don't love you. I don't want to be with you."

He didn't move. Didn't say a word, but something in his eyes danced. "I understand."

What she wouldn't give to hear him say he loved her. What she wouldn't give to be in his arms right now. Safe. Warm. What she wouldn't give to feel his lips on hers one last time.

Amy lowered the dryer even more.

Cosette jerked. "I am here with my *daughter*."

The young woman paused and slightly shifted.

"She's all I care about. So please go."

Amy glanced at Cosette. "Mommy, do you mean that? You'd make him leave?"

"Of course," Cosette said, holding back tears. "I don't love him. I don't want to be his partner. Have his back. Rely on him. I don't want to have babies with him or grow old with him."

Wilder's face crumpled and his jaw worked hard.

"You're all I need, Amy. Please unbind me and let me out of this tub. We'll go away together forever."

Amy stepped back a foot, lowered the dryer. "Really?"

"Really." Cosette glanced at Wilder.

Amy caught it and raised the dryer. "I knew you were a liar."

Wilder pulled the trigger.

The hair dryer dropped.

TWELVE

The hair dryer clattered on the tile floor next to the tub. Wilder's heart pumped as he moved quickly and unplugged it.

Amy fell, knocked her head against the toilet and crumpled in a heap, unconscious. He hadn't taken a kill shot, only wounded her. "Beckett! Call the police and an ambulance."

Wheezer rushed inside and grabbed a towel, kneeling and applying pressure on Amy's shoulder wound. Wilder didn't fault him for it.

"Get me out! Get me out! Get me out!" Cosette screamed, now hysterical and panicked.

Wilder cut the ropes on her feet with his knife, then hauled a bound Cosette from the water and into his lap on the bathroom floor.

"Wheezer, let's get Amy out of here and into the hall-way," Beckett said and lifted the wounded woman from the floor, closing the bathroom door on Wilder and Cosette.

Wilder grabbed a bath towel from the rack and wrapped it around Cosette while he cut her hands loose. Seeing her in that tub and knowing any second she might die had scared him more than anything in his entire life. "You're safe now. You're safe."

Cosette let out a strangled sob and collapsed against him, snaking her arms around his neck. Her skin felt like ice.

"Let it all out, darlin.' And you *are* my darlin'. Period." All the fear, the grief, everything she couldn't show in front of Amy poured out against his chest. "You were a brave soldier." He stroked her wet hair. "Smart." There was so much he wanted to say, but now wasn't the time. "You did good. Real good," he murmured. "Now just cry it out." She continued to wail, her shoulders shaking, body shuddering against him. She clutched his shirt and mumbled something incoherent.

Sirens reached his ears. "We're gonna go home in just a bit, okay?" And by home he meant CCM. She could let the lease go on that stupid apartment. "Just you and me and a red velvet cake."

She sniffed and nodded against his chest. The woman must be exhausted, but she'd held it together like a pro. He gripped her and stood, and with her cradled in his arms, walked downstairs into the living room, where the Carson family minus one were being attended to by first responders. Jody stayed with them. Detective Bodine stood by the door, ready for the real story.

"Can you stand, baby?" Wilder asked.

Cosette nodded.

Wilder lowered her, but kept his arm around her. "Does she need to do this now?"

"I can do it," she said. "I want to do it, but first…" She went to Mrs. Carson and they hugged and cried. "I'm so sorry. I wish I could have done more. This is my fault."

"No, it isn't. It was that crazy woman's. You saved us. Thank you." The paramedics led them to the ambulance and Cosette walked with her.

Wilder's chest swelled with pride. This was the woman he wanted to spend his life with, but once again he'd have to wait a little longer, and he could.

He'd been waiting his whole life for Cosette.

"You gonna do the deed?" Evan asked.

Wilder chortled. "What deed is that?"

"Marriage, you idiot." Jody wrapped her arms around Evan. "You *lo-o-ove* her," she teased and snickered.

"I'm not loving *you* right now." But he grinned at his team. They'd been there to pull him up. To love him unconditionally. To fight with him and for him.

And right now, one of them was deeply wounded.

"I'll be right back." Wilder stepped outside.

Wheezer stood in the middle of the lawn, staring up at the stars, lost as a goose.

"It was Christmas Eve and I was seven," Wilder said. "I couldn't sleep that night, waiting on Santa to bring me presents. I wanted to see him. Talk to him. So I waited up behind the couch and long into the night, I heard rustling. I peeped over the couch and do you know what I saw?"

"I know it wasn't Santa."

"It was my dad. Eating the cookies and drinking the milk. I didn't want to believe it. At first, I thought he was sabotaging Christmas. What would Santa think when he showed up to crumbs and an empty milk glass? But then my mom brought in our gifts and I watched them fill our stockings with candy."

Wheezer faced him, moisture in his eyes.

"The people we love can fool us the easiest. Our eyes are blinded to them. What we think is real…isn't sometimes. I was so mad on Christmas morning, I refused to open the gifts and participate in the festivities. Santa was a lie. And I was mostly mad at myself for believing. All the signs were there."

Wheezer wiped his eyes. "The girl I fell in love with murdered five people, used me for information, manipulated, lied and nearly killed Cosette! I didn't believe in a fairy tale, I believed in love."

Wilder did something he didn't typically do. He went to Wheezer and embraced him. "You can always believe in love. But you can't believe lies that crop up when you're hurting. Lies like it's your fault. Brother, don't do that." He sighed. "Don't give up all the gifts that are before you because you're mad at yourself. Don't stop participating in festivities because you're angry and bitter. You'll miss out."

Wheezer hugged him back, with zero shame. Wilder gripped him hard. "No one blames you. We love you, man, and we'd be lost without you."

"Thank you, Wilder." Wheezer finally broke the embrace, sniffed and nodded. "Thank you," he said, before heading back inside.

Wilder was exhausted. For the first time he was feeling it in sore muscles and burning eyes.

Cosette strode toward him. She'd changed into dry clothes, though her hair was still wet.

"How did you find me?" she asked.

Wilder drew her to him, never wanting to let her out of his sight again. "A lot of digging. Almost murdering your colleagues." He chuckled and kissed the top of her head. "But the truth is it was your father, Cosette. Leon."

Cosette reared back, eyes wide. "What? He was involved in this?"

"No. Not exactly." He explained what had happened and what the lawyer had really wanted. "If I hadn't answered…" He didn't even want to think about it.

"Five months. I could have known this five months ago!" She cried again as she leaned into him.

"Hindsight, darlin'. Hindsight."

A few moments later, she looked up. "Wilder. I need to see him."

* * *

Cosette sat on a blanket by the burned-down stable. The breeze lightly stirred the sweet scent of honeysuckle.

Two days ago, she'd visited her father in prison. She wasn't sure what to expect. He'd looked so old and feeble. But his eyes were strong. Dad had shared with her how he'd received salvation and how Jesus had changed his life. He, too, had regrets, but there was no changing what had happened. He'd shed many tears, as well.

She wasn't planning on becoming BFFs with him, but she planned to visit on occasion, and she'd set up a debit card plan to accept his collect calls from her cell phone. It would be tough. She forgave him, but she hadn't forgotten, and she was human. Emotions needed to be worked through on a daily, sometimes hourly, basis. But it was a start.

Wilder had given her some space these past few days, and while she appreciated it, she wanted to know what he was thinking. But he was a private man. Sometimes slow to move, and she loved him, so she'd love him even for that and be patient. He'd understood her subtle message to him; she'd seen the light bulb go on in his eyes. He'd told her she was always his darlin' and he'd called her "baby."

But he had yet to profess his love.

He'd yet to kiss her again.

"Hey," Wilder said and moseyed up to her blanket. "Can I cop a squat?"

"Your property." She smirked and patted the blanket.

He sat beside her, his thigh brushing hers, sending a spray of joy into her middle. "When I was three, my dad told me I was a man. That I had responsibilities to take care of my baby sister. Then when Caley was born, that fell to me, too. I took it seriously, Cosette. The year before Meghan died in my arms—"

"What?" Meghan had died in Wilder's arms?

"Meghan. Allie. Two women I cared about. And I almost lost you." She listened as he shared his heart. The secrets he'd held inside so long. "I didn't do couch sessions with you because I was afraid you'd get in my head and pull that out."

"I would have, but thank you for telling me on your own. Finally." She sighed as if she was sad. "What will we fight about now?"

"I'm sure we'll come up with something." He tucked a strand of hair behind her ear.

Cosette gazed at him. "Wilder, I think it's time for us to stop being afraid of what the other one might think and just lay it all out there."

"All right. If we're putting it all out there." He framed her face. "I love you. I've loved you for most of the years I've known you. I never said anything because to love you means to give you all of me. And I was afraid if you knew about my failures, you'd think differently of me and that...that would kill me."

He. Loved. Her.

She soared to the highest heavens.

"I know now that's not true," he said. "So if you want me, Cosette...then I'm all yours. Every single part. All the emotion you want and can handle."

She grinned, but he cut her off before she could utter a word.

"But you need to know something." He took her hand, kissed her knuckles. "When I say I'm yours, I mean it. I belong to you. And if you love me, too, then you belong to me. Not as a possession. I don't own you. But you *are* mine. I'll take care of you always. And you'll take care of me. Even if it means dragging me from burning buildings." He chuckled. "Though I'll likely still yell at you for it."

Cosette couldn't love this man more, but... "How can you say *if* I love you, too? I told you I loved you first."

Wilder's sly grin sent ripples through her. "No, you said you *didn't* love me. You didn't want to have my babies." Yearning burned in his eyes and seared into hers. "You said you didn't want to grow old with me," he whispered.

"I lied. Maybe I did it too well. I am, after all, a behavioral expert."

"Hmm." Wilder nuzzled her cheek.

She belonged to God. And she wanted nothing more than to belong to Wilder Flynn. "I do love you, Wilder. And I belong to you."

"Well, that's all I needed to hear." He pecked her cheek and pulled away. "But you need to hear one more thing." He pulled a red velvet box from his pocket and switched to a kneeling position. "Cosette, will you marry me? Because I really don't want to go on through this life without you in it. By my side. As my wife and partner. The only woman who can touch my hair."

She cackled. "I do love your hair."

"Me, too, but let's focus."

She snickered again and tears rushed to her eyes. "Yes! I'll marry you."

He placed the gorgeous emerald-cut diamond on her finger, then cradled her face and gently kissed her. Almost chaste, but she could taste the emotion behind it, the intensity of his love for her and the peace of knowing she belonged to this man till death did them part.

EPILOGUE

May, the following year

Wilder slipped behind the new stable and sneaked up on Cosette, snaking his arm around her waist and whisking her into one of the empty stalls. She squealed and laughed as he butted her up against the wall.

"What are you doing?" she asked.

"Stealing a kiss from my wife before all the hoopla starts." This coming July marked the anniversary of their first year as a married couple. It had been every bit as awesome as Wilder had expected.

During the year, Cosette had worked tirelessly to rebuild the stable and open the equine therapy practice. Six horses. A private office and drive. The fencing had been done and Mercy Abrams had flown out to help them with the details. Today was a private grand opening with friends and family to celebrate this accomplishment.

A baby's cry echoed in the distance, but Wilder ignored it and let himself get lost in Cosette's kiss—this woman who belonged to him.

The crying continued and grew closer.

"You have to learn when Daddy says no crying, he means it. Yes, he does." Beckett Marsh was baby-talking to his squalling son, and Caley and Shepherd had announced they were expecting. Wilder hoped Cosette didn't get the bug too fast. He was enjoying having her all to himself.

But sometimes when Beck's son wasn't wailing, he itched for a few babies himself.

Cosette smothered a snicker at Beckett's baby talk, and they crouched low to not get caught. "I also wanted to tell you that your dad is here," he whispered.

He'd been released on parole four months ago. They weren't close by any means, and Wilder was pretty sure Leon was okay with that and understood, but he was here for this, and they'd let him video call into the wedding to watch.

Beckett had given Cosette away.

"See, that's better. No crying," Beckett cooed.

"Are you in here *demanding* our son not cry?" Aurora stomped into the stable, and Wilder and Cosette peeked over the stall wall. "Have you learned nothing being married to me?"

"Possibly," he said in a teasing tone.

Maybe Wilder should clue them in on the fact they weren't alone.

"And I'm not demanding anything other than some teething gel and a bib. The slobber is off the chain," Beckett said.

"Have you seen Caley?" Shepherd swaggered into the stable. "I can't find her."

"She was puking in the guest bathroom twenty minutes ago. The smell of hay made her sick," Aurora said. "That'll pass."

Shep scrunched his nose. "Not soon enough," he muttered.

Wilder covered Cosette's mouth to stifle her laugh, and when that didn't work, he shoved her into the hay and kissed her again. That shut her up.

"Anybody seen Wilder or Cosette?" Evan's voice boomed across the stable. "The caterer is looking for her. Which reminds me, I'm starving. Can we order a pizza and not tell Cosette? Who wants to eat froufrou food? It's not a tea party."

Jody's voice sounded. "The photographer is here."

Since they'd all be dressed up, they were having new team photos taken for the Covenant Crisis Management website. Cosette included. She was still part of the team. He'd tossed his policy on not dating—or marrying—employees.

"We should stop making out in the hay and tell them we're in here. Besides, Evan needs to know I did not order froufrou foods."

"No way." Wilder picked hay from her hair and helped her sit up. "And yes, you did," he whispered. "They're all doll-sized. We're grown men. We don't eat doll food."

She made the pouty face he adored.

"I smell them," Jody said.

He inwardly groaned. He wanted five more minutes alone with his wife.

Jody popped her head over the stall door and grinned. "Making out in the hay."

"I hate that sniffer!" Wilder teased and helped Cosette to her feet. "And it's our stable. We can do what we want."

"You might wanna pick the straw out of your hair before our photo," Shep said. "Just an observation."

Cosette huffed, and she and Wilder went to work doing so.

"Y'all! Y'all!" Caley came running, huffing and puffing, her face pale.

"Quit running," Shepherd growled.

"I'm pregnant, not helpless." She shrugged off his remark. "Wheezer's here. With a date!"

He'd been more himself lately, since Roger Renfrow had been doing some counseling with him.

Cosette had invited the Carson girls to come for equine therapy. She'd also sweet-talked Wilder into building small guest cabins for patients and their families who needed to come from out of town. He'd never be able to say no to her.

"A date?" Wilder asked. "Bring her into the control room. I want to give her a lie detector test before this goes any further." Wilder was half joking. At some point you just had to get back in the saddle and trust again. In people. In God.

He trusted this team—this family—with his life. And now that he didn't feel the need to carry everything on his own shoulders, he could lean on them for support. He'd finally realized leaning on friends and God didn't make you weak. It made you strong.

He put his head on Cosette's and she hugged him to her. Wilder had never felt stronger.

* * * * *

If you liked this story from Jessica R. Patch,
check out the rest of
THE SECURITY SPECIALISTS *miniseries:*

DEEP WATERS
SECRET SERVICE SETUP

Available now from Love Inspired Suspense!

Find more great reads at www.Harlequin.com

Dear Reader,

I have enjoyed writing this series, especially Wilder's story. From the beginning, I knew he was going to be a complicated character, but one I believe many of us can relate to. To feel comfortable, he has to control every situation and outcome. When he can't, he feels weak and afraid. The truth is, none of us have supreme control and we have to rest in the knowledge that God alone does. And I think that boils down to the trust factor. Do we truly trust Him in all situations? Can we trust Him to work everything out for good? Can we trust Him when the reports are bad? I encourage you (and myself) to spend some time in prayer and ask God to help us see areas where we can surrender to Him and trust Him to see the outcome through—then trust Him with that outcome! I love to hear from readers. Please email me at jessica@jessicarpatch.com and sign up for my newsletter at www.jessicarpatch.com and get "Patched In" to new releases and book news/deals.

Warmly,
Jessica

Get 4 FREE REWARDS!

We'll send you 2 FREE Books <u>plus</u> 2 FREE Mystery Gifts.

Love Inspired® Suspense books feature Christian characters facing challenges to their faith... and lives.

FREE Value Over $20

SPECIAL EXCERPT FROM

Love Inspired.
SUSPENSE

*When Chase McLear is accused of aiding the Red Rose
Killer, can Maisy Lockwood, the daughter of one of
the victims, help him clear his name before they both
become targets?*

*Read on for a sneak preview of
STANDING FAST by **Maggie K. Black**,
the next book in the **MILITARY K-9 UNIT** miniseries,
available July 2018 from Love Inspired Suspense!*

The scream was high-pitched and terrified, sending
Senior Airman Chase McLear shooting straight out of
bed like a bullet from a gun. Furious howls from his K-9
beagle, Queenie, sounded the alarm that danger was near.
Chase's long legs propelled him across the floor. He felt
the muscles in his arms tense for an unknown battle, as the
faces of the brave men and women who'd been viciously
killed by Boyd Sullivan, the notorious Red Rose Killer,
flickered like a slide show through his mind.

Sudden pain shot through his sole as his bare foot
landed hard on one of the wooden building blocks his
daughter, Allie, had left scattered across the floor. He
grabbed the door frame and blinked hard. His three-year-
old daughter was crying out in her sleep from her bedroom
down the hall.

Seemed they were both having nightmares tonight.

He started down the hall toward her, ignoring the stinging pain in his foot.

"No!" His daughter's tiny panicked voice filled the darkened air.

"It's okay, Allie! Everything's going to be okay. Daddy's coming!" He reached her room. There in the gentle glow of a night-light was his daughter's tiny form tossing and turning on top of her blankets. Her eyes were still scrunched tightly in sleep.

A loud crack outside yanked his attention to the window at his right. He leaped to his feet and started for the glass just in time to see the blur of a figure rush away through the bushes. His heart pounded like a war drum in his rib cage as he threw open the window. The screen had been slit with what looked like a knife and peeled back, as if someone had tried to get inside

He closed the window firmly, locking it in place. Then he looked down at Queenie. "Stay here. Protect Allie."

Don't miss
STANDING FAST by Maggie K. Black,
available July 2018 wherever
Love Inspired® Suspense books and ebooks are sold.

www.LoveInspired.com

Looking for inspiration in tales
of hope, faith and heartfelt romance?

Check out **Love Inspired**® and
Love Inspired® **Suspense** books!

New books available every month!

LIGENRE2018